SHERLOCK HOLMES

AND

THE MISSING SHAKESPEARE

/ / / /

J.R. RAIN
& CHANEL SMITH

THE WATSON FILES

Published by
Crop Circle Books
212 Third Crater, Moon

Printed in the United States of America.

ISBN-13: 978-1546319245
ISBN-10: 1546319247

Chapter One:
A Great Discovery

'Elementary,' he said. 'It is one of those instances where the reasoner can produce an effect which seems remarkable to his neighbor, because the latter has missed the one little point which is the basis of the deduction.' —Sherlock Holmes

The simplicity with which the details of this latest case fell into place was not particularly unusual but it had amazed nonetheless for it.

Even now, as I think back to the mystery of the Missing Shakespeare, I am hard pressed to comprehend all the fine details of how my friend, Mr. Sherlock Holmes, had ever managed to unravel some of the key evidence surrounding the matter. At the time, I had chalked up a lot of his cursory deductions to his in-depth knowledge of the British aristocracy; the man is a veritable walking glossary for *Burke's Peerage, Baronetage and Knightage*. It was only later, as I put pen to paper to transcribe our adventure in my journals, that it occurred to me just how he'd done it.

Backward reasoning was what Sherlock called it; the ability to recreate a sequence of events which produced a result.

In my reverie and my renewed admiration for Mr. Holmes, I was taken back to how I'd completely and unexpectedly met my dear friend and colleague all those years ago. Some might even say *randomly*, but not Holmes. No, he believed quite rigidly that everything meant something, everything had a purpose for happening or existing.

Apparently our purpose had to do with adventures and mystery. And murder. Oh, the many murders!

Our choices in life lead us down many roads. And sometimes we are quite hard pressed to decipher the destination... Ah! But those are the times when we should try to enjoy the journey the most!

Indeed, my own convoluted road had been leading me to Sherlock Holmes my entire life, and I would have it no other way.

***

I cannot now recall the exact date I dropped by Baker Street.

It was a typical English summer day, though, with the rain lashing down in copious amounts. I had been visiting a patient close by when the rain broke and, knowing I would always have a welcome at Baker Street, I made the detour to escape the downpour.

The housekeeper opened the door and allowed me entrance to the hallway. I gave her my drenched coat and proceeded upstairs to the study, where I knew I would find my old friend.

"How goes it, Watson?" Holmes asked before I even entered the room.

Opening the door, I found Holmes in his usual chair, turned toward the fire, the chair preventing him from seeing the door.

"How did you know it was me, Holmes?"

"Who else could be coming in at this hour of the day... and in the middle of this torrent?" He looked around at me and smiled. "And the sound of those big regimental boots of yours that you persist in wearing when trudging around town is quite distinctive."

"Ah." That was the only answer I could muster in response to his conclusion.

"Sit yourself down, Watson," Holmes said. "You ought to take advantage of the fire and get yourself dry before you catch a cold."

"Thank you, Holmes." I made my way to the other side of the fire where my usual chair was placed. From that vantage point, I immediately observed Holmes was holding something on his lap. "What is that you have there, Holmes?" asked I.

"It is a missing play by the Great Bard himself."

"Shakespeare?" I asked, perplexed by the curious string of words uttered by my good friend. "And did you say missing?"

"Who else? And yes."

"Are you absolutely sure, Holmes?"

"Indeed, my dear Watson. It came to me today, and I am quite sure of its authenticity. As it turns out, I just happen to know a thing or two about the old boy."

I blinked, digesting this news, and looked again at the bundled manuscript that lay on my dear friend's lap. Holmes's long, white fingers held the document delicately. Meanwhile, the fire crackled and popped in the hearth, and the occasional, mischievous gust of wind blew the curtains out like lilac ghosts.

"But how did you come by it, Holmes?" I asked, quite perplexed. "And whoever heard of a missing Shakespearean play, anyway?"

"It was a bit of a mystery."

"Which you have already uncannily solved?"

"Of course, Watson."

"Well, Holmes, do not leave me on tenterhooks. What is the mystery?"

"*Was* the mystery, Watson; it has already been solved."

"You are being as elusive and frustrating as ever, Holmes. Very frustrating indeed."

He placed the palms of his hands flat against the manuscript and tapped his boot to some unheard music. "Patience, Watson. All in good time."

"Come, out with it, Holmes," I said in slight agitation. "The least you can say is how you came about having it."

"All shall be explained to you in due time, my dear friend." Holmes smiled and looked up at the ceiling, closing his eyes. He put his fingers together, resting his elbows on the armrests of the chair. "That is, about an hour after we have indulged in our evening tea, I should say. We are, of course, proper gentlemen."

I sighed. "Of course."

Chapter Two:
In the Presence of a Lady

True to form, it was nearly sixty minutes to the second after we had finished our tea when there came a knock upon the door downstairs. The rain had stopped pouring down by then, having slowed to a steady drizzle. A minute later, the soaking figure of a woman appeared in the study. Obviously, she had borne the brunt of the storm.

Holmes jumped up to grab a plaid blanket and wrap it around her shoulders before guiding her into the room to take my seat by the fire. I myself had gotten up to greet the lady and was happy for her to take the chair. I sat down on the windowsill.

"Watson, Miss Harcourt. Miss Harcourt, may I introduce you to my dear friend, Doctor Watson," Holmes said as he introduced us.

"A pleasure, Miss Harcourt," I greeted her.

"Likewise, Doctor Watson," she said, still shivering.

Holmes sat down again, allowing a sizable interim in which Miss Harcourt could rediscover herself. Eventually, she found her damp clothes had dried a bit and the fire had warmed her enough for her to speak. Even so, as she spoke, I could see steam coming from the bottom of her silk skirt and from the lace that framed the ends of her sleeves. Her black leather boots, too, were still drying, a testament of which was the way the steam rose from the laces.

"Did you manage to find out more about the manuscript, Mr. Holmes?" she asked.

Holmes smiled and nodded seriously. "I have indeed been able to authenticate the document for you, Miss Harcourt. It is truly a work by one William Shakespeare, though certainly not his finest stuff."

Miss Harcourt smiled, too, at that analysis. "Indeed, it is not, Mr. Holmes. It is quite an early play of his, don't you agree? Perhaps he was still finding his feet, so to speak, in the world of the stage."

"That might just be the case, Miss Harcourt. The handwriting itself is consistent with that of his earliest works. Tight, rigid, thoughtful, unlike his hastily written later attempts, genius as they were. Yet his youthfulness is not the most interesting thing about this whole affair. Can you please, for my friend Watson's sake, recount how you came about this splendid document?"

The young woman turned to face me and I was struck by the clear, blue color of her large, almond-shaped eyes. Her face was perfectly angelic too and the strands of dark hair that came out from underneath her hat glowed as though they were made of the same sort of fine silk that formed her skirt.

"I worked as a governess at Galham House last year, you see."

"My God, you were there when the tragedy happened?" I exclaimed in surprise. The drama that took place at Galham House had been splashed all over the papers for months. The master of the house had lost his mind, it seems, and killed his wife and his children, then put a rope around his neck and jumped from the mezzanine overlooking the entrance to the house. The penny dreadfuls had had a field day of their own, twisting the local people's imaginations with gruesome crime scene pictures and equally fantastic stories.

She nodded and looked down sadly for a moment. "A great tragedy it was. Those poor little ones were lovely, and innocent of anything. They did not deserve the pain they'd been dealt."

"And, pray tell, what did you proceed to do after this unfortunate incident?" asked I, once a suitably respectful moment of silence had passed. "I believe the new Earl of Galham has no children, so a governess would not have been required at the house."

Miss Harcourt nodded and gave a vague smile. "I call myself 'miss,' but my proper title would be Lady Jessica Flora of Harcourt and Avon."

I had to think for a moment and saw the vague smile on Holmes's narrow face. I gathered he had discovered that by himself not soon after he had first been introduced to the lady.

"You might want to read up on the English Peerage, Watson," he interjected happily. "Burke's Peerage is worth perusing."

"My father is the Earl of Harcourt; my mother is the Countess of Avon. When her brother died, she inherited the title. It is I who will inherit those titles upon the demise of my parents."

"If you are an heiress of these two titles and estates, why were you working as a governess?" I asked, still not quite understanding the nature of her employment.

"My father did not want me to live the sheltered life many heiresses lead. Indeed, he has been careful to educate me well and send me to some fine higher learning establishments. He also insisted I find employment instead of supporting myself by means of a stipend he gives me."

"A wise decision on your father's part, Miss Harcourt," Holmes said. "It means you will be far more knowledgeable about the world when you come to manage those joint estates, rather than having to leave it to a steward or your husband."

"Quite so, Mr. Holmes." She turned back to me

and continued her tale. "The Galhams and the Avons have always had a very close relationship seeing as their estates border each other. The families often had to collaborate on matters of land ownership. My mother was childhood friends with the then earl, Lord Roger's father, and arranged for the position there for me." There was a pause as she sipped her tea before continuing. "As you know, Galham House is not far from Stratford-upon-Avon, the home of our cunning bard. It was rumored that Shakespeare himself spent some time in the house when it was first built."

"He did?"

Holmes chuckled. "Shakespeare was notorious for his amorous appetites and the Earl of Galham had a number of rather pretty daughters, in addition to a very suitable wife."

Miss Harcourt, too, grinned. "It was lucky for his poor wife, Anne, that they moved to the city in the end. He was discreet enough, but Galham House proved far too seductive for the love-struck young William. Indeed, his advances on Lady Anne Galham, the youngest daughter of the earl and the fiancée of Lord Lucy, could have proved his undoing. Especially when it was discovered she was with child."

"By Shakespeare?" I demanded in utter surprise.

"We do not know, but that would seem to be the case." She shook her head. "But I digress. I was about to tell you how I came by the manuscript, not about my family's history."

Just as she was about to launch into her narrative, the housekeeper came in with a tray containing cups and a pot of tea, alongside a plate of biscuits. Holmes took it from her and set it down upon the table, pouring each of us a cup in turn.

Having sipped the warm beverage, Miss Harcourt started her account of the procurement of the manuscript.

"After the tragedy at Galham House, I stayed on until the late earl's brother came to take charge of the estate. The servants, too, stayed on in that interim. The new earl dismissed several of them of course, as he has no children and keeps his residence here in London, where he has his own staff."

"But why did you stay there?" I asked her, being quite curious. "If your mother is the Countess of Avon, does your family not keep an estate nearby?"

Miss Harcourt blushed at the question. "My mother does own Bridgewell Abbey, the ancestral seat of the Earls of Avon, and she owns some residential property in Stratford-upon-Avon as well as in the surrounding villages. She is also the owner of the Pen and Sword Inn in said town. She offered to put me up at the house and at the inn in turn, but I had my reasons to stay. Reasons I could not divulge to my parents."

"Your fellow employee, Mr. Miller." I did not need Holmes's help to understand that. "I thought your father was progressive?"

"Not *that* progressive," she smiled. "Mr. John Miller is after all only a lowly gardener and I wanted to stay with him for as long as possible. I could possibly have gotten him a job at one of our estates afterward. But again, Doctor Watson, I digress now.

"In the interim between the tragedy and the arrival of the new earl, we had the run of the house to ourselves. The atmosphere among the staff was still professional, but standards were a bit more relaxed than they had been. I think we all needed to let our hair down after the terrible events of the preceding period. Mr. Miller and I took to strolling around the grounds and around the house. He had his work to perform, too, but there was nothing to stop me from accompanying him in the grounds and in the hothouses.

"On one occasion, exactly five days after the tragedy and two days before the expected arrival of Earl Reginald, we were in the library. I had been studying the books there, having nothing else to do, and Mr. Miller came to find me there. I had, of course, had ample time to study the books previously, as I had taught the children, but now I was looking through the section containing plays and fiction. I was surprised to find the earl or the countess had purchased every single novel of Jane

Austen's, which was a good start for me to distract myself from the events in the house. Mr. Miller was a better distraction, of course, when he arrived." She blushed again, this time brighter. "It was also he who found there was a book in the wrong place. Among the Jane Austen novels was one book in particular, its cover black and the spine lined with gold thread. It was untitled. I pulled it out a little and found it was a copy of Shakespeare's *Tempest*. I pushed it back in its proper position, but Mr. Miller said he could not abide it being in the wrong place. He proceeded to take the book out to place it with the other Shakespearean works. However, it did not come off the shelf. Instead, when he pulled it out far enough there was a click and a section of the shelf came forward. Behind the shelf was a small recess. Mr. Miller reached inside it and took the manuscript in question out.

"I examined it and thought at once it was a previously undiscovered Shakespearean play. I wanted to present the finding of it to the butler and to the new earl, Lord Reginald. Mr. Miller convinced me not to, that my top priority was first to keep the manuscript safe and, once safe, to take the steps necessary to ascertain its authorship. With the utmost discretion, of course."

"Of course," said I. "So you came to find Mr. Holmes for such a service?"

"Not exactly," Miss Harcourt said hesitantly. "Shortly after the discovery of the manuscript, Earl

Galham dismissed me officially to travel anywhere. A day earlier, he had also dismissed Mr. Miller, as had been somewhat expected. I am ashamed to say that I appropriated the manuscript from the premises at that time."

"You stole it, you mean?" I interjected.

"Yes. Yes, I suppose I did. Mr. Miller had put it into my head that it was only safe with me, and I began to believe him."

"Very well," I said, now straight on the facts. "Continue."

"Well, not a week later, I received a letter from Mr. Miller reminding me to have the manuscript examined. I fully intended to, but hadn't yet formulated a plan. After all, how does one do such a thing? Anyway, I never heard again from Mr. Miller after that. Two weeks later, I engaged Mr. Holmes, who had been referred to me by a friend, to find out all he could about this manuscript, and to, perhaps, bring me back into contact with Mr. Miller."

She blushed again, mightily, in fact.

"And this, my dear Watson," Holmes interrupted, "is where the mystery lies that I have solved."

With one of his self-assured and knowing smiles, Holmes turned to Miss Harcourt. "I will call on you at four o'clock two days hence at Harcourt Hall."

"How did you know where I was staying?" she asked in surprise.

"The two times you came to call on me, you got here at a quarter past six. It takes a lady of your stature approximately sixteen minutes to walk here from Waterloo Station; the train from Dover arrives at five minutes to six. That train passes the station of Penstone Heath, two miles from Harcourt Hall. If you had come from Stratford-upon-Avon you would, of course, have arrived here an hour earlier."

"Truly an astounding feat of deduction, Mr. Holmes," Miss Harcourt commented.

"One needs only a working understanding of how train schedules work—"

"She is paying you a compliment, Holmes," said I.

"Ah." And my good friend bowed formerly. "I thank you."

Miss Harcourt studied my friend for a good twenty seconds before responding. "But I am confused, Mr. Holmes. You say you have solved the mystery, but why do you insist on keeping me in the dark about it?"

Holmes nodded, and said, "Because I have solved the mystery, but I have not yet procured the solution to your problem."

Chapter Three:
Unlikely bedfellows

"What was that, Holmes?" I demanded of my friend when Miss Harcourt had departed for Harcourt Hall.

"What was what, Watson?" Holmes returned the inquiry casually as he prepared his pipe.

"'I have solved the mystery but I have not found a solution to your problem?'"

"Ah, that is indeed the case, Watson." Holmes grabbed the tongs and took an ember from the fire to light his pipe. "I have solved the mystery of the manuscript, I am already aware of Mr. Miller's role in it and where he might be located, but none of it helps Lady Harcourt." He turned to me then, blowing out a large cloud of smoke. "Would you care to accompany me in my investigations, Doctor Watson? I assume you have time to spare in the next two days?"

"Uncanny, but you are right again, Holmes. I have no appointments; I have only rounds to make. My wife is away to visit her sister in Scotland, so I am completely at your disposal."

"Excellent, Watson. I will see you at Waterloo Station at ten o'clock in the morning. If you visit old Mrs. Jacobson at the end of your round, you would only be five minutes away from the station."

I decided not to question how Holmes knew my rounds, and I did not ask him why he reckoned I would be calling on Mrs. Jacobson the next morning as I had received no word of her being unwell. Instead, I just bade him farewell.

By the time I left the Baker Street residence, the rain had stopped and the streets were nearly empty, making for an easy walk home.

***

As I was having my morning tea, a footman arrived with a message.

Curious, I opened it at once to discover a request to visit Mrs. Jacobson that morning as she had been taken ill during the night. I shook my head, less over the news of Mrs. Robinson's failing health, but more over Holmes's seemingly supernatural ability to predict the future. I promised I would call on her and proceeded to do so, as on Holmes's suggestion, at the end of my rounds. I then went on to Waterloo Station, where I found

Holmes waiting impatiently on the platform, conversing with the conductor of the train to Dover.

"Honestly, Watson," he exclaimed exasperatedly, "You are a full minute late. Do make haste and board before Mr. Evans here decides he will not wait a second longer."

I did so instantly, recognizing that my good friend was in one of his moods, and was followed by Holmes into the compartment. He had not closed the door before the conductor blew his whistle and the train was set into motion.

"We are going to Harcourt Hall, I presume?" I inquired of Holmes, wishing to circumvent his ire.

"We are not, Watson," Holmes said not-so-gently.

"Then might I inquire where we are going?"

"You may."

I waited for a moment but received no answer, which I promptly pointed out to him.

"Oh, you were inquiring with the presupposition that an answer would also be forthcoming."

Having confirmed that sentiment, I saw Holmes smile and recline into the seat, resting his elbows on the armrests and placing his fingertips together again, closing his eyes and not opening them again until the train had reached the village of Penstone Heath.

We alighted from the train there and Holmes proceeded rapidly from the station into the village. I marched quickly but found it hard to keep up with Holmes's long strides.

We walked through the village without a stop and we turned onto a country lane without a word. After some minutes of steady walking, I saw the imposing figure of a country estate come into view. I assumed it was Harcourt Hall and our destination.

Almost a mile away from the estate, though, Holmes pointed to a side road that joined the lane there, cutting a gap between the willows that lined the lane. "That's the road to Harcourt Hall," Holmes proclaimed, although he continued along the lane to quite a different estate in front of us.

I blinked and missed a step. "Harcourt Hall? But I thought that was where we were headed."

"No, we are going to call on their neighbor, the Marquis of Tach Saggart."

"The Marquis of Tach Saggart?" I had not heard the name before.

"Yes, that is his estate, Clonmore House." Holmes gave a chuckle of laughter. "The Marquis is a member of the Irish Peerage. Rather a delusional one, though. He is a descendant of Lord Fitzwilliam, one of the commanders of the army that was comprehensively thrashed by the O'Byrne clansmen at the battle of Glenmalure."

He glanced back and, undoubtedly, correctly read the puzzled expression on my face. In his pleasant voice, he launched into a verse of a song he must have picked up on one of his forays into the

Irish expatriate community in London. Holmes had the uncanny ability to retain the lyrics and melody of any song he'd ever heard.

"From Tach Saggart to Clonmore, there flows a stream of Saxon gore, and great is Rory Óg O'More at sending the loons to Hades. White is sick and Grey has fled, now for Black Fitzwilliam's head, we'll send it over dripping red to Liza and her ladies."

He looked round at me again and smiled. "That battle did not go well for the present Englishmen and collaborators. Yet in true form, honorable titles were issued to the deceased commanders and then passed on to their descendants. The Marquis of Tach Saggart took pride in where his ancestor earned the title and named his house after the place."

"It is a new house?" I asked, making a leap of logic.

"Indeed, Watson. It was built ten years ago. The family was extremely impoverished and moved to the Ohio River Valley, as many of their countrymen solved their hunger and monetary problems by joining the Royal Navy or the armies on the Peninsula or in India. The current marquis is the second generation to have been born in the United States of America. That may explain his naivety about his heritage. The family procured some property there and got by. It was the current marquis, Gerald Fitzwilliam, who began working as a ranch hand in Texas after the war between the States and worked his way up the ranks. He became a foreman at a young age and his talent helped him secure a very favorable marriage. He made a small fortune from the cattle trade and invested most of that setting up further cattle ranches in Argentina. Subsequent investments also paid off and some ten years ago the marquis bought a house in Portobello, Dublin, took his place in the Irish Peerage and proceeded to build this house as well."

"A remarkable man then," I stated, quite impressed.

"Indeed, Watson, indeed."

"But why are we going to see the Marquis of Tach Saggart?"

"Why Watson, we are not."

I blinked at that and must confess I was baffled by Holmes. This would not be the first, nor the last.

"Then who are we calling on, Holmes?"

"We are calling on Mr. John Miller of course."

Chapter Four:
A Robbery

When Holmes dropped the knocker on the oaken door of Clonmore House, it took several moments before anyone showed up to open it.

I took my time observing the surroundings, as Holmes had shown me how to do many times. The pillars of the door frame were made of concrete painted white to resemble marble, the doorsteps were the same. I drew the conclusion the house had been built in a hurry and on a budget, though it certainly was not without significant value. The garden was well cared for and I noticed the grass had only recently been cut. I assumed Mr. John Miller had been hired as the new gardener by the Marquis and we were seeking permission to find him on the grounds.

Yet, the moment the butler allowed us entrance into Clonmore House, Holmes demanded to see the master's son, although my good friend did not wait for the butler to show us to his young master; instead, he brushed past the man and went straight up the stairs.

The winding stairs that led us to the second floor of the impressive domicile were made from oak which seemed to have matured in the ten years since it had been installed. In alcoves along the steps were placed busts, which I took to be images of the ancestors of the family. On the third floor of the house lay a plush carpet and the walls were lined with portraits and paintings. They were perfectly aligned and not one was out of place. The walls were spotless and the windows overlooking the lawn had been cleaned that very morning. I could still smell a whiff of rubbing alcohol.

At the end of the hallway, Holmes halted. He knocked on the door. A strong voice bade him enter. I went in behind him and saw a young man reclined on a chaise lounge. He had a book in his hands and was looking up at us.

"Good day, Mr. Fitzwilliam," Holmes greeted him. "I am Sherlock Holmes; this is my associate, Doctor Watson."

The man rose and offered us each his hand to shake in turn.

"Gerald Fitzwilliam," he introduced himself. "Your fame precedes you, Mr. Holmes."

"Thank you, Mr. Fitzwilliam." Holmes gestured to a sofa by the large bay window. "May we?"

Not waiting for a positive answer, Holmes plunked himself down in the plush velvet covering of the sofa. I sat down next to him.

"To what do I owe the honor of your visit, Mr. Holmes?" Fitzwilliam began. "I sincerely doubt such a famous sleuth would be calling on me without good cause."

"We are looking for a Mr. John Miller, former gardener at Galham House." Holmes smiled then.

I knew by the delicate shade of crimson in the face of young master Fitzwilliam that we had come to the right place.

Holmes continued, "Your father holds similar beliefs as Lord Harcourt, I imagine."

Young Fitzwilliam nodded. "He does not exactly approve of marrying within the peerage either. He has an American heiress lined up for me to wed."

"Did you know Miss Harcourt before taking up the job at Galham House?"

Fitzwilliam shook his head. "I did not. I had only seen her from afar, never met her or spoke to her."

"How is that possible? You live so near to each other, there must have been ample opportunities to meet," I demanded of him, interrupting the conversation between Holmes and him.

"I spent my childhood in America and Ireland and then most of my time here I have been at Eton and at Cambridge."

"How does a Cambridge man end up as a gardener at Galham House?" I blurted out, beside myself with curiosity.

Fitzwilliam gave a wry smile. "Business is rather dull work. I suppose I am good at it, a talent I must have been born with, but I do not enjoy business. Simple tasks please me much more. Obviously, I could never allow a lowly position like that under my own name, so I took an alias."

He got up and poured himself a double measure of whiskey at the well-stocked bar located in a corner of his room. He poured the contents of his glass straight down his throat and returned to his seat. "As you are already aware of my alias, Mr. Holmes, I then I assume you are making these inquiries in regard to the manuscript Miss Harcourt and I discovered?"

Holmes nodded. "You knew instantly it was written by William Shakespeare."

"I did." Fitzwilliam smiled. "I studied him extensively at Cambridge. I even managed to lay eyes on some original handwritten documents. I recognized the handwriting immediately."

Holmes said nothing for a while. He did not have the frenzied look he tended to have when working out a problem. I had to remind myself of his claim of having solved the mystery already.

Eventually, Holmes got up.

"I do implore you to speak to your neighbor's

daughter and reveal your true identity. She is quite worried about young Mr. Miller. And it is obvious that you care deeply about her."

"I assume I exhibited all the characters of a man in love?"

"You did," said Holmes. "And then some."

Mr. Fitzwilliam smiled meekly and rose to shake our hands again. "I shall, Mr. Holmes."

We made our way back to the station to catch the train back to London, but Holmes decided we could catch a later train and guided me into the Penstone Arms Inn across from Penstone Heath Station.

A helpful hostess seated us in a corner of the pub for a rather well-prepared lunch of roast beef and some very good ale. We entered into a conversation about the various affairs that had kept us both busy over the past month, and all the reasons we had not been able to see more of each other. It seemed Holmes had spent a lot of time solving quite a few uninteresting cases. It was not often he wasted time on those, but it seemed there had been a surprising lack of challenging crimes and mysteries in the last few months, causing him to take up such cases for financial reasons.

***

It was just as we were finishing up our tankards of ale that a boy stormed into the pub. He raced to the bar and asked something of the barkeeper who in turn pointed in our direction and the boy came up to our table.

"Mr. Holmes?" he asked timidly.

Holmes nodded as a confirmation.

"I have a telegram for you, sir."

"Thank you, my boy."

Holmes fished in his pocket for some sort of monetary reward for the messenger. He ended up handing the boy a sixpence piece, which was rather gladly received. It was a significant reward for a few minutes' work. The boy looking completely dumbfounded was of no surprise.

Holmes read the telegram and his face betrayed a look of shock. He shot up from his chair, gave me the telegram to read and went at once to the bar to pay for our luncheon.

The telegram was from Holmes's housekeeper. It read:

"As I was out not half an hour ago, someone entered the premises. There is nothing missing, bar the manuscript you have been researching."

I folded the telegram up, put it into my jacket pocket and rushed after my friend.

Chapter Five:
A Candle in the Window

We arrived back at Baker Street with Holmes in a rare, frantic mood.

He raced up the stairs and into his study. He looked over the place carefully, knowing his housekeeper would have taken care not to disturb anything more than was necessary to establish what was missing. Despite his frantic mood, he looked like a bloodhound with his nose down, tracing the scent of his quarry. He scoured the place for any clue of who might have been there to relieve him of the precious manuscript.

"This was no ordinary heist I fear, Watson," he remarked in the end. "Someone knew exactly what he was looking for and possibly even where it was to be found. He was in and out without leaving a single trace."

"Not a trace?" I asked. "It's quite impossible to

have found no trace at all."

"Indeed." Holmes grimaced and plopped down into his chair. "There is no sign of the doors being forced, or the window. There are no footprints, nothing to suggest anyone's presence in this room at all."

"Then how did he do it?"

Holmes frowned and grumbled, "That, my dear Watson, is a mystery I would dearly like to solve at present."

***

After having completed my rounds, I visited Holmes again the next morning only to find him balancing on the roof of the stables located behind his Baker Street residence.

"What, by Jove, are you doing up there, Holmes?" I exclaimed when I first spotted him there through the open window.

"Eureka!" he exclaimed in turn, before jumping for the window frame. He pulled himself up with a great effort and came into the house again. "Well, I have discovered the point of entry, Watson."

"They came through this window via the stable roof?" asked I. The window was in an unlikely spot. Indeed, it took all of Holmes's physical prowess to make the leap from the roof and pull himself into the house.

"Several roof tiles were out of place and there

were markings on the window ledge. This window is often unlocked. The key word is 'often.'"

I nodded. "Because sometimes it is locked, too."

"Of course, Watson. After all, who better than we to know that crime is alive and well in London? Regardless, sometimes we are lazy, and I myself would never have guessed a thief to be so bold as to utilize this high window."

"Did he get lucky?" asked I. "And come at the right time, when the window happened to be unlocked?"

Holmes cocked his head. There was sweat on his brow. I suspected he had been searching for clues all morning and afternoon. "Perhaps, perhaps not. A good thief would have ascertained when the window was left open, though it would have taken a long time of careful study to conclude which window would be left open, and at what time."

I blinked. "How long?"

Holmes shrugged as he dusted himself off. "To thoroughly case this residence, to understand which windows might be left unlocked, and at what time, would require at least one week of careful study." Holmes looked down at his big, now dirty hands with a displeased frown. He removed a clean handkerchief and begun rubbing his palms meticulously.

I gaped. "But that would be since the moment you were given the manuscript."

"Indeed, my dear Watson."

"The thief has been lying in wait this entire time?"

"It would appear so." Holmes returned to the study and replaced the handkerchief with the meerschaum pipe, in which he began stuffing with tobacco. He lit it and sat down in his chair. "Of course, that would have required a veritable amount of determination to have spent a week looking over every part of this building to determine a way to enter unseen, to know where he could locate this document and how best to go about getting it without any circumvention," he mused before taking a long pull on his pipe and blowing a big cloud of smoke toward the ceiling.

I took my usual seat and looked at him carefully. "Was there more than one person involved?"

"There was," Holmes said. "A lookout surely. And I shall determine who played me this prank. Of all the criminal acts, the one I can least abide is the burglarizing of my own home."

I could not help but grin at Holmes's slightly conceited statement. "If there is anything I can do to help clarify this case, I will keep myself at your disposal."

"That is very kind of you, my dear friend, but I fear we might not see each other for a short while."

"Why would that be, Holmes?"

"As I shall have to travel in different circles

and different places to get to the bottom of this."

I spent the rest of the day in Holmes's company, until such time as I knew the train from Newcastle would arrive. Then I sped to Paddington station to pick up my wife, leaving Holmes with only his cryptic description of what he would be undertaking.

With the ministering angel of domestic bliss back in residence, I returned to my normal schedule without ado. I went to look in on Holmes at Baker Street several times over the next few weeks, but I was told each time Holmes had not returned. It would be a month until I saw my friend again.

Chapter Six:
The Valet

"Hello, would you mind waiting a moment?"
Holmes shouted at the tanned man who, in other
circumstances, would not have been so
conspicuous.

There were so many light-skinned servants in
the city of London at the time that they practically
went unnoticed for the most part. The trend of
keeping on the exotic servants from the colonies
had taken hold in the city as returning diplomats
from India, the West Indies and merchants from the
Americas brought their endeared house staff back
to England with them.

He'd always thought it a product of their
lingering taste for the exotic but would later realize
the truth of the matter was that English servants of
distinction had a tendency of being even more

snobbish than the aristocrats they were used to serving. It struck him as being tremendously ironic.

Mr. Paul Kijumbe was just such one exotic servant brought to England by none other than Countess Mary Galham's father after his safaris in Eastern Africa. He was a member of the coastal Swahili tribe from the village of Nyali near Mombasa. The ancestral intermarriages between the Swahili people and the Arabs who frequented Africa's eastern coast had resulted in a population who bore striking resemblances to the quadroons and octoroons of the Southern regions of the American state of Louisiana.

As Kijumbe stood at the bar among his fellow valets and a few footmen from other distinguished London households, Holmes couldn't help but overhear their conversation. Paul was quite boisterously describing some of the strange errands he ran for his current employer.

"As utterly bonkers as some of this stuff is, it sure does beat working for that stuffed shirt, Lord Sutton."

A-ha! *Holmes thought.* I do believe I have you now!

He sat patiently in a corner of the public house sipping a single pint of Irish stout until I noticed the group begin to break up. They were mumbling about getting back below stairs ahead of the ringing of the evening gong. Quickly enough, Paul made his way to the door and out to the street.

Holmes was close behind him.

"Hello, would you mind waiting a moment?" he called.

The man continued walking down the street, blatantly ignoring Holmes's call for him to wait.

"Wait there! I have something I'd like to discuss with you! It's related to a business venture and it would be worth your time, I swear!" he shouted again. Holmes believed the man's name was Kijumbe and that he had a very good idea what happened to the Shakespeare manuscript which had been stolen from his flat.

The man turned into an alley which connected the street he was on to the next street over. The avenue was more crowded, and would allow the man to lose Holmes much faster. Holmes picked up his pace barreling into the entrance of the alley. In quick secession, several things happen all at once. Holmes had been about to take his next step when he suddenly found himself flat on his back; all the air had been struck from his lungs.

I should have expected that, *Holmes thought.*

Before he could have another cognizant thought, the man he had been pursuing was straddling his chest, raining fists into Holmes's ribs and face. Holmes planted his feet and thrust his hips upward; trying to buck the man off, but his assailant was an experienced fighter. He did not have his weight directly on Holmes's chest. Instead, he was balanced on the balls of his feet to keep his weight forward and himself more stable. The position allowed him to react quickly when Holmes tried to throw him off, and that meant that Holmes was at a distinct disadvantage. The bucking motion, Homes had made, was intended to bring him to his feet; atop his assailant. However, since his assailant was able to rise and avoid all but a glancing blow from Holmes's legs, the next punch he threw did double the damage. His fist slammed into Holmes's face and the downward momentum of Holmes's failed bucking move slammed his head into the cobblestones.

His vision blurred and he heard the man laughing. Holmes was not sure how, but he still maintained consciousness. He managed to land a kick to the inside of the assailant's left knee, and the man buckled; his laughter became a grunt of pain. The man launched a haymaker at Holmes's head, but Holmes managed to slide slightly out of the way. The fist connected with the cobblestones in a meaty crunch. Holmes knew that his assailant was more infuriated than ever.

This is not the time for honorable tactics, thought the detective.

And thus, he brought his knee up into the man's groin. The man's grunt of pain turned into a high-pitched squeal. Holmes used the momentary distraction to slide out from underneath the man and shift in behind him, from where he delivered a punch to the back of the man's head.

SHERLOCK HOLMES
AND THE MISSING SHAKESPEARE

Holmes was now certain the man was Kijumbe; based on descriptions he had gathered. The man he believed was Kijumbe turned and flailed with a blind punch that Holmes deftly knocked aside. The problem with a blind punch, however, is that they are normally followed by a punch that is much more precise. This was no exception, and Holmes took Paul's fist directly to the stomach. For the second time that day, Holmes had had the wind knocked out of him.

As he doubled up over his aching stomach, the man swung at his head again. Holmes turned, and felt the fist meant for his chin slide harmlessly down his cheek. The detective gathered himself and landed three swift punches to Paul's face. Paul staggered upright and swayed uncertainly on his feet. He lurched toward Holmes, arms outstretched, and Holmes delivered a punishing uppercut to the man's jaw. His feet, Holmes would swear till the last breath, left the ground and Paul landed flat on his back; with a whoosh and a crunch. He moved slightly and Holmes delivered an unforgiving heel kick to his jaw to finish him off.

***

A boy came rushing into my practice that evening, asking me to attend to a patient forthwith.

A man had collapsed in the street. As it was only two streets away from me, I was asked to attend to him. I immediately grabbed my bag and followed the boy toward the scene of the incident.

Arriving there, I found a small crowd of concerned citizens hovering over the fallen man, who lay on his side. I instantly crouched down beside the man and began examining him. I noticed no trauma or any mark that would explain his collapse, forcing me to conclude it had been illness or blood pressure to cause his collapse. I took his pulse and found he was alive, but not conscious.

At that moment, the boy pointed out the man who had sent him to seek me out. The man was a tall and thin, dressed in fine clothes, with large sideburns and a mustache. He had reddish hair, which was slightly longer than it should possibly have been to be entirely fashionable. But it was the eyes that betrayed him to me. I almost ejaculated his name in surprise, but a wink from those eyes stopped me doing so.

"Can you help him, Doctor Watson?" asked the disguised Sherlock Holmes.

"If someone can halt a Hackney carriage, we can get him to my practice and I shall help him further there."

A cab was signaled and Holmes and I got the man into it. Moments later, we reached my practice and we placed the man on a table in one of my rooms.

"He will come round in half an hour, without your aid, Watson."

"Did you do this to him, Holmes?"

Holmes nodded. "I needed to go through his pockets. I might be a dab hand at the art of picking pockets, though admittedly slightly rusty, but I cannot pick all his pockets at once. So instead, I injected him with a sedative, allowing me to bring him here, to the privacy of your humble practice in order to pilfer what he has on his person."

"But what are you looking for, Holmes?" I asked as Holmes began rifling through the man's clothes.

"His keys," Holmes answered briefly.

I hoped to assist him by fishing a ring of keys out of his left trouser pocket, but Holmes ignored them and kept looking. It took him a good five minutes to open the man's shirt and find there was a small key on a ring that had been locked into his nipple.

"Well, I would never have found that by picking his pockets," he ejaculated cheerfully.

"That is a very odd thing to do."

"Indeed it is." Holmes carefully unlocked the ring, like one would an earring and slide the key from it. He then locked the ring again. "I knew he had the key on his person, but this was quite unexpected, even for me."

"What does that key do?"

Holmes laughed. "Why, Watson, it opens a lock."

"But what lock, Holmes?"

Holmes touched the side of his nose again. "All will be revealed to you in due time, Watson." He drew some bank notes from a pocket of his jacket and lay them beside the man on the table. "This should cover your expenses, Doctor. This man should not have to pay for them and I will not be around when he comes to."

"But where are you going, Holmes?"

Holmes pulled his figure straight, adjusted his jacket and pushed his hat at a jaunty angle. "That too will be revealed to you in time." At that moment, he chose to adopt a posh accent, usually only used by the upper echelons of London society. Then he tapped his hat with his cane in greeting or goodbye and promptly marched out the door.

***

A week after this affair, I received a message from my friend, asking me to join him in Stratford-upon-Avon at the nearest opportunity I chanced to have. I thus told a colleague I would be taking a day off, informed my wife and, two days later, having made all the necessary preparations, I undertook the journey to the hometown of the Great Bard himself.

As per Holmes's instruction, I took a room at the Pen and Sword Inn. I was pleasantly surprised by the quality of the accommodations there, but I was less pleased to find no trace of Holmes.

I took an excellent luncheon there and then

remained in the common room where I read. I had brought some medical journals for the trip, knowing that I would have the chance to read them at least on the train, if not while waiting for Holmes, which I seemed to do entirely too much. I thus sat quite happily, though impatiently, in a corner, reading up on experimentations and studies in my profession, drinking tea, and later in the afternoon, ale. As the sun began setting over Stratford-upon-Avon, I ordered some food for dinner, hoping Holmes would show up soon. I had reached the last of the journals and I feared boredom would get the better of me if my friend would not grace me soon with his company.

It was only as I finished this last journal and began drinking the hot chocolate I had ordered that a familiar frame folded itself through the entrance.

The hat was gone, as were the posh clothes. He was once again in his usual attire and it was easy to see he was more at ease without the disguise he had adopted. He sat down at my table and hailed the waiter for an empty cup. The moment it arrived, Holmes poured himself some hot chocolate from my steaming jug.

"I am truly glad to be myself again. I can spend months pretending to be the scum of London, but trying to mix with the peers of the realm, the rich and the famous and all their varying offspring, is a job I would rather leave than take."

"Is that what you have been doing, Holmes?"

He grumbled something and drank some of the beverage from his cup. "The underworld is my domain, but the underworld cannot tell me where this manuscript is. Nor could it tell me where the men came from who burgled my abode."

"So you traversed the upper classes?"

"Indeed."

"And did you find what you were looking for?"

Holmes grimaced then. "I believe I did. Though I have yet to test that belief."

I left that statement unquestioned; knowing Holmes's testing of his theories and knowledge would eventually involve yours truly. Instead, I queried him on the contents of the missing manuscript.

"Why, Watson, it is a missing play by William Shakespeare," he exclaimed.

"I am, of course, aware of that, Holmes. But I was wondering as to the play itself. Perhaps you can relay the tale it tells to me."

Holmes gave a vague smile. He poured the last of the hot chocolate into his own cup and ordered some more for my sake. Having taken another sip, he launched into the tale.

"Costarde is an old man already when he is sent from France to be the new ambassador to the court of the King of Spain. He has always been unlucky in love, constantly betrayed or simply unsuccessful in finding a suitable marriage partner. In Madrid's Escordia Palace, he meets Maria. She is of a noble family; her father is chamberlain to the King of Spain, Don Ciprian.

"He falls hopelessly in love and begins courting her, but her father prevents him from continuing his pursuit of her. He sends her away to their country estate and arranges a match with Don Lorenzo. As the eldest daughter of an ancient family, she is expected to marry into another Hidalgo family, descendants of those knights who fought the Moors.

"She goes through a short courtship, as is customary of course, and then prepares to marry Don Lorenzo. But it is then that Costarde finds her and continues his courting of her in secret. She responds and they become secret lovers. Of course, Don Lorenzo finds out, as does her father, and Don Lorenzo challenges Costarde to a duel. Instead, Costarde retreats to Madrid, but Don Lorenzo pursues him there and it is quite obvious he will never let him off.

"Costarde writes a short comedy ridiculing the whole situation and Maria performs it with her sister Anna and her friend at a party thrown in honor of Don Lorenzo's arrival in Madrid. Don Lorenzo sees the error of his challenge, but his honor will not allow him to stop pursuing Costarde. He seeks him out in private, slaps him and says his honor is now satisfied.

"They then find Don Ciprian and Maria and they agree Maria will marry Don Lorenzo, who does love her sincerely. Costarde is heartbroken, but cannot agree to anything else without facing another challenge from Don Lorenzo and subsequently from Don Ciprian. He says his goodbye to Maria and prepares to resign his duties in Madrid. As he writes his letter to the King of France begging to be relieved of his position, Anna, Maria's sister, comes to his chambers and confesses to him she has admired him from afar all this time. She begs him to reconsider withdrawing from Madrid and they begin a courtship. Don Ciprian is happy for the match to take place, to marry his second daughter to a wealthy French nobleman. They wed on the same day as Don Lorenzo and Maria and they all live happily ever after."

Holmes gave a small bow and I clapped my hands heartily. "A fine tale, indeed," said I.

"I imagine Shakespeare and Thomas Kydd drew on each other for the names and setting. They probably came to blows over it."

"It sounds a familiar story."

"I also imagine Shakespeare drew heavily on his affair with Lady Anne Galham for his inspiration," he said airily. "Luckily, this is a comedy and not a tragedy."

"That would seem likely."

"But, my dear Watson." He brought his hands down on the surface of the table. "You have been studying all day and I have been busy all day. I reckon it is time to retire and pick up the trail in the morning."

"The trail?"

"Yes, the trail. You did not think I would ask you to come here if I did not need your assistance in tracking down whoever is at the heart of this case?" With that, he rose and he went up the stairs to the room he had engaged.

Chapter Seven:
Old Friends

"I need you to run an errand for me, Watson," Holmes said over our breakfast.

I blinked at that but agreed to do what he asked.

"There is a notary here in town. I want to see the will of Lord Galham."

"The current earl?"

Holmes frowned. "It would seem to me to be elementary that I meant the will of the previous earl."

"How do you propose I go about that?"

"I believe Mr. Kendricks, who is the junior partner of the notary firm of Jennings and Kendricks, is a brother of a friend of yours. Your natural charms should win his confidence."

"Winning his confidence does not equate to

him breaking the confidentiality of his profession and showing me the will of a respected member of society."

"I have full faith in you, Watson."

Holmes did not divulge any further details to me, instead leaving me to my own devices the rest of that day.

And so I sought out the office of Mr. Kendricks, only to discover that Holmes was right, as he usually is. Llewelyn Kendricks was the younger brother of Rhodri Kendricks, a Welshman in whose company I had spent many a happy hour. He had been a coal merchant and settled in London for a while before returning to the Black Hills. I had visited him at his Black Hills residence and he had told me in passing that his brother, Llewelyn, had taken up a position as a solicitor in London. Of course, this was many years ago.

Drawing on my acquaintance with Rhodri, I made my announcement and was received by Llewelyn Kendricks. He offered me tea and we sat and talked for a while.

After an hour, I questioned him on his knowledge of the Galham family and the tragedy that had taken place at Galham House.

"You know, it was, in fact, the old earl who interceded and helped me get this position," said the younger Kendricks.

"Was it now?"

He nodded. "Lord Galham was a good friend.

We met in London, at the Welsh Society."

"The Welsh Society?"

"Lord Galham's mother was the youngest daughter of the Marquis of Pembroke. He spent many a month in Wales as a child and he was always fascinated by the history, the language and the culture. The only place close to the center of power to speak the Cambrian tongue was at the Welsh Society, and it is thus we met. We became close friends and spent rather a lot of time together. When his father passed and left the estate to him, he retired to run the house and the estate. I think he felt lonely, and as I was still looking for a steady position in London, he interceded to get me this job."

"You would not rather have stayed in London? It seems a country notary is not the same as a position in the city."

"I would, but I decided the security of this position would be preferable over a lower position in London and the uncertainty that often goes with it."

"And being close to a friend, I take it?"

Kendricks smiled. "And that too."

"Is there not a Mrs. Kendricks?" I asked him then.

He looked down and shook his head. "Alas, no. It, therefore, has been rather lonesome here since the tragedy that shook us all to the very cores of our beings. All I have had to distract me from the tragic loss of my friend is my work and that is hardly a suitable distraction all the time. And unfortunately after several years, I am still essentially a stranger here. An alien, so to speak."

"I can understand that. My wife hails from Berwickshire and still often feels an alien in London. It must be worse still in a country town like this."

***

After our conversation, Mr. Jennings, his business partner, came into Kendricks's office and invited both of us to supper with him and his wife. I tried to decline, but I could not do so gracefully and thus accepted.

I left Kendricks for a few hours, allowing him to complete his business for the day and allowing myself to enjoy the old town of Stratford-upon-Avon. I bought a hat for my wife and found one shop that sold excellent stockings, which I also obtained for her. A bookshop provided me with some more reading material for that evening, including the local newspaper. I returned to the inn for a while to have some tea and then joined Kendricks again.

Together we walked to the edge of the town, where he resided. A boy opened the door and, upon recognizing Kendricks, he let us in. He led us through the house to the parlor. His father, Mr.

Arnold Jennings, was seated in his chair in the sitting room at the back of the house. The parlor was an unusual room, as one wall was nearly taken up by an entire window, but I could see why it had been constructed in such a manner. The room faced south and was flooded with light. The view was of their sizable garden and the river beyond. I remarked upon it and Jennings graciously and smilingly accepted the compliments.

"Some stately homes have rooms like this, but it is rare the middle classes will have such a design. I invested a fortune rebuilding this part of the house, but it was worth every penny."

"When did you have this done?" asked I.

"Only in the last two months. Some investments of mine worked out rather well and after a little conclave with my wife, we decided this would be a marvelous way to spend the money."

"It is indeed," I replied. "My wife would dearly like to have a room like this in our own home. I doubt, however, it will work as well in London as it does here."

Jennings smiled. "Indeed. Maybe it will work in Chiswick or Twickenham though?"

"Ah, but that would require even more good fortune to relocate to such towns."

Kendricks and Jennings both laughed and it was then the maid came to summon us to the dining room.

Mrs. Jennings and Jennings's boys and

daughter were waiting there. The table was wonderfully laid out with a roast, roasted vegetables and potatoes. It was a meal that made my mouth water immediately, as it was a rare treat to find this bounty in the center of London. Even with the income of a doctor, as I had the fortunate disposal of, access to this kind of fresh country produce was very limited.

The conversation over the meal inevitably turned to business and of course life in London. Mrs. Kendricks was quite interested in the social affairs of the city, the gossip of town and what was currently in the theater. The latest play I had seen was a production of Marc Anthony and Cleopatra at Drury Lane and she was quite keen to hear about it, even if the play itself must have been well known to her.

At the end of the meal, the maid servant brought in a trifle, which was consumed with relish to the last spoonful. Mrs. Jennings and the children then retired and Jennings produced some excellent brandy and choice cigars.

"You do have a superb taste in tobacco, Jennings," remarked Kendricks.

"A gift from Lord Galham, Kendricks."

"You are close with the new earl?" I inquired of Jennings.

He nodded, blowing out a large cloud of smoke. "We have known each other for quite a while. Reginald and I went to Sunday school together, right here in Stratford-upon-Avon. They, of course, were taught by a governess and tutors, but their mother insisted they attend local Sunday school. Reginald and I, being the same age, we became fast friends."

"Why did she insist on that?" Kendricks demanded. "Does Galham House not have a chapel?"

"It does, but Lady Edith, the Dowager Countess Galham, is the daughter of a parson. She insisted the family attend a service in the town church every week." Jennings grinned. "Though there was a rumor about it at the time that she did so for less than holy reasons."

"An affair?" I asked.

"With Reverend Jones, yes."

Kendricks blinked. "Reverend Jones? The retired minister? Does his land not border the dowager's?"

Jennings touched his finger to the side of his nose and said no more.

***

With the brandy and cigars finished, we had coffee and as the night fell over the town, Kendricks and I quitted the house and each went our way, agreeing to meet for lunch the next day. When I returned to the inn, I found Holmes was not there.

I spent an hour in the common room to read the

day's newspaper while enjoying the inn's fine ale. With the newspaper read, I made to retire to my room but just as I began to climb the stairs, Holmes entered the inn and waved at me the moment he noticed me there. As I turned and made to descend again, Holmes ran up and took me by the elbow. "Shall we partake of something in the privacy of my parlor, my dear Watson?"

I agreed, although quite filled up with fine food and liquors, and while I waited there upon the step, Holmes darted down to ask for a tray of something to be brought up to his room. He then marched up after me with his long strides.

"I will not ask you about your progress," Holmes said the moment we entered his room, "as it is still early days for you."

"You wished to talk to me in the privacy of your room to tell me that?"

Holmes let out a chuckle of laughter. "You are right, of course, in thinking I have an ulterior motive in wanting your presence here."

"What would that be, Holmes?"

"I need your professional opinion on a matter of great importance."

There were a table and some comfortable chairs by the window, so I sat down there. A moment later, there was a knock on the door and a maid brought in a tray with brandy and coffee for us. She placed it on the table and went out again after Holmes told her to add it to his tab.

Holmes sat down and pulled a folder from the inner pocket of his coat. "Some subterfuge allowed me to obtain this from the local pathologist."

"What is it?"

"The report he gave to the coroner investigating the deaths at Galham House."

I balked at that comment. "But, Holmes, why are you looking into that?"

"In due course, Watson, in due course."

"But, by Jove, Holmes!" I ejaculated. "Surely you do not think the tragedy at Galham House is related to the manuscript's theft?"

"I am of that mind."

I did not know how to respond to that, so instead I took the folder from him. I opened it and began to leaf through the pages contained within. "I will need some time to read through these, Holmes."

"Take as much time as you need, Watson. I am quite patient."

"You are? Am I still really speaking to the great and honorable Sherlock Holmes?" I teased him.

Holmes grinned and waved the comment away. "We are getting closer to the truth of this case, Watson. I feel it."

I held up the folder. "And you think my opinion on the pathologist's report will get us even closer?"

"It is a piece of this puzzle, my dear Watson.

The more pieces I manage to place in the right position, the clearer the picture will get." Holmes sat down, too and began stuffing his pipe. "I doubt any single piece that is missing will cause me to be unable to see what the puzzle depicts, but every piece I can put into place is one step closer to the goal."

"Normally you are keen to determine every detail, Holmes."

"As many as possible, Watson. Deduction can uncover many other details that remain hidden from us. As long as we have the details in place to come to the right conclusion."

I took up the first page of the report and began to read as Holmes lit his pipe and began contentedly puffing away.

The first pages contained the details on Sir Roger, Earl Galham. The pages were held together by a wire slipped through a round hole punched into the top left-hand corner of each sheet. The next pages concerned his wife, the Lady Mary, Countess Galham. The names of their children were written on a separate pathology report, of which was not included.

I scanned the details and found the pathologist had been very thorough, which caused me to have an acute sense of admiration for his work. Yet it had been a long day and the brandy was taking a stronger hold over me than the coffee was. I felt my eyes slowly closing and I had to shake myself awake.

"I say, Holmes, perhaps I should read these over breakfast."

Holmes took a sip of brandy and then continued smoking his pipe. "I dare say it is best left to a moment when your mind is capable of processing the data, as you rightly determine. But I trust you will stay for another few moments?"

"Though the brandy is excellent, I must confess I am rather tired."

"Then perhaps I can persuade you to stay by telling you something about my exploits of the day?"

"I thought you were not going to recount those?"

"No, Watson, I said I would not say anything regarding why I am looking into the tragedy at Galham House."

"Though of course, Galham House is where the manuscript was found."

"Indeed."

"But you think those deaths are related to the manuscript's discovery and subsequent theft from your rooms?"

Holmes gestured with his pipe. "You know the answer to that question already, Watson. You need not ask it, for that is the question to which you will not receive an answer. Not yet."

I held my tongue for a moment, taking some brandy. "Well then, Holmes, of what did you undertake this day?"

So Holmes began his recount of the day's events.

Chapter Eight:
Hot on the Trail

"The one person we have ruled out as being the perpetrator in the theft of the missing Shakespeare manuscript is, of course, the Honorable Sir Gerald Fitzwilliam. Yet he was there when it was discovered and he was the reason we were away when the manuscript was taken. I thought it prudent to discover as much as I could about his whereabouts while he was John Miller at Galham House.

"As John Miller was the gardener at Galham House, I started my investigations at the stores that sell supplies for gardening. There are a number of farmers who remember him, asking for manure to be delivered to the grounds. They all relayed the same really. John Miller was a very competent gardener, who knew exactly what he was doing. They also all wondered about his voice. He was not a local and his accent was something they could not quite grasp. He managed to hide the foreign accent in his voice for a part, but they all noticed the poshness in his speech.

"The general store and the blacksmith next door reported much the same. They recalled an unremarkable man who was a splendid gardener with the same oddities in speech and voice. The blacksmith also recalled that our man had ordered a ring to be made out of a piece of steel he provided. He never picked it up, for the next day, the tragedy at Galham House occurred.

"I also asked the blacksmith about a key in my possession. I did not think he would recognize it, but he did. He recognized it as his own work. He explained it to be the key to a strongbox he had constructed for a gentleman."

"What gentleman?"

"Alas, I do not know."

"Did he not give a name?"

"He did. John Smith."

Soon after Holmes's short tale, I retired to my rooms. In the morning, I took the pathologist's report with me to my breakfast. I inquired whether Holmes was already having his tea or would care to join me momentarily, but the innkeeper told me Mr. Holmes had already left.

Holmes's peculiar departure held my interest for only a few moments before I settled down at a table in the main hall and asked for the breakfast menu.

As soon as the pot of tea arrived, I opened up the pathology files again and read through the last reports. I was fascinated as I read deeper into the documents and was relieved that I had started with the reports instead of the crime scene photographs.

It seems that Lord Galham had, for all intents and purposes, lost his mind that night. He'd strangled his wife, Lady Mary, to death in their bed and then slit the throats of both his children with a hunting knife. Finally, Lord Galham threw himself off the balcony with his neck tied in a noose and hanged himself to death.

I was appalled and yet strangely intrigued. I couldn't help but wonder what could have gone so dreadfully wrong that a well-respected, wealthy peer of the realm would murder his family and then kill himself. As I'd deduced earlier, he must have been squarely out of his mind.

When my soft boiled egg, sausages and toast arrived, I was well ready for the refreshment. I threw the files shut, pushed them aside and turned my attention to the meal. As I swallowed the last bite of toast and lifted the teacup to my lips, I was hit with a very important question.

I placed the cup back in the saucer and threw open the file; searching with everything I had to find the clue I needed. Alas, it wasn't there.

"Oh, by George! I think I've found it," I said to myself, but loud enough to warrant a raised eyebrow or two.

It didn't take me long to get myself together and leave the public house. I gave the boy there a sixpence coin to hail a carriage for me while I stopped at the desk to send a telegram to my wife. I had to let her know that I would not be staying in Stratford-upon-Avon any longer, having been abandoned by Holmes. I only planned to do one last thing before catching the early afternoon train back to London.

When the cab pulled up, I boarded it and asked the driver to take me to Llewelyn Kendricks's office as quickly as he could. At that point, it was all I could do to hope that my new friend would share my concern in the matter and help me get closer to the bottom of things.

I followed his clerk into the office and found Kendricks seated at his desk pouring over a pile of legal documents. As the clerk added even more files, he announced my arrival to his employer. It was apparently Kendricks's morning for doing his work as a notary and he was fully engaged in cross-checking several facts before affixing his stamp and signature to the paperwork in each docket.

I cleared my throat, having realized he had not heard a word his clerk had said to him regarding my presence in his office. Finally, he glanced up, looking a bit harried, and waved me in. I took a seat across from him at the desk.

"I'll wait until you are finished, my friend," I

started. "As what I have to tell you, and, even more so, what I wish to ask of you, are two very serious matters indeed."

"I dare say, Watson," he replied without looking up at me, "it all sounds like extremely grave business."

"You wouldn't even be able to guess the half of it, old boy."

"Then you will appreciate some tea while you wait. I promise it won't be long; you've rather piqued my interest."

Kendricks called for a pot of tea to be brought in, as it was close to ten o'clock. A proper time for tea indeed. When it arrived a few moments later, steaming and fragrant, there were sandwiches and cakes along with it. I hadn't realized I was hungry until I spotted the sandwiches. Ham, smoked salmon and egg sandwiches were perfectly complemented by tomato, cucumber and watercress selections. In contrast, a lighter fare had been selected for the sweet portion; it was only morning tea, after all. Still, I was quite delighted to see all of my favorites: lemon cake, madeleines and raisin scones. I immediately left the armchair in front of my friend and took a seat at the card table where the tea and food tray had been set up.

The smell of a delicious meal must have put some fire under the otherwise overwhelmed Kendricks because it wasn't long after I'd swallowed my third sandwich that he placed his stamp down heavily on the desk, flourished the last signature and called for his clerk to come and clear away the pile of dockets.

He took the seat across from me and immediately began to fill his plate with sandwiches. I poured the tea while he made his selections, then waited patiently for him to polish off a sandwich or two before I began to speak.

"Well, by now you must be wondering why I barged into your office so early this morning without even so much as a prior appointment, Kendricks," I started.

"Indeed, the thought had crossed my mind, Watson. But I, by no means, consider your company to be an inconvenience. It's actually quite lovely to have a reason to get away from the desk and take a proper mid-morning break, for once," he replied graciously. "I am curious, though, I'll admit."

"I'll get to the matter at hand then," I obliged. "Yesterday, I came into possession of the pathologist's reports from the deaths of the late Lord Galham and his family and I have happened upon a few of the doctor's observations that concern me."

"The pathology reports? How did you…"

I put up my hands in protest to stop him from continuing along that line of questioning and simply stated, "I have my resources, Kendrick." He nodded his acceptance of my explanation and lifted his teacup to his lips, waiting for me to proceed.

"I found that the doctor had not pursued an explanation of the signs I noticed and I could only surmise that at that time, he may not have recognized them or had the resources to proceed with the proper testing."

Kendricks's face revealed that he was intrigued with what I had to say, so I decided to give him a few clues. If I were to expect the man to help me in the manner I needed, he would have to get a better feel for where I was going in the investigation.

"I noticed there was a white residue around the mouths of Lord Galham, Lady Mary and the children. Also, their lips bore a slight bluish tinge." Kendricks was at a loss as to the meaning of my observation, as any layman would be, so I explained further. "It seems that they may have been forced to inhale chloroform, perhaps from a rag soaked in the solution then placed over their nose and mouth. It would have, at the very least, put them in a very drugged state and, at the worst, completely rendered them unconscious."

An expression of comprehension spread over the lawyer's face and a grin played at the corner of his lips.

"And you say that Roger's body also exhibited these signs?"

"Indeed, good sir."

"But that would mean that he was as much a victim as the rest of the family unless the unlikely happened, which would be that he drugged himself."

"Precisely!" I said and continued to sip my tea.

"You think someone murdered his family and then killed Roger in an effort to frame him for the crime?"

"Dead men tell no tales, Kendricks."

We sat in silence for a few minutes. The words sank in slowly as we drank our tea and moved on to the sweet treats on the cake stand. Finally, he asked, "But what has that all to do with me, Watson?"

"That, dear sir, is the winning question!" I replied, jumping up from my seat with excitement. I may have been overplaying the suspense a little bit but I had to. What I was about to ask Kendrick to do was quite close to bordering on an illegal activity. But I hoped he would now feel driven by his conscience to provide a solution to the mystery. "You were the custodian of the late earl's will, were you not?" Kendricks nodded cautiously. "I suspect that the contents of his will may have been altered to name a different beneficiary than he had originally intended. If that is indeed the case, then we would have true motive for the crime and a clear line of sight to the perpetrator."

He shrugged. "So, how do I come in?"

"I would like to see the original will and testament of the late Earl of Galham."

"And I would have loved nothing more than to show it to you but it is no longer in my possession.

Not even a copy."

"What? How is that possible? Were you not the man's sole solicitor and your father before you?"

"Indeed. However, it is the right of the executor of the estate that, once the will was read in an open forum for all the family to hear, to retain the document and that's exactly what Reginald did. In fact, he retrieved the will from me in its original sealed state some three days before the date set for the reading. As there was nothing out of the ordinary in its contents and it was quite in line with the usual inheritance practices, I had not even seen the need to keep a copy."

I pondered on that for a moment and suddenly it hit me like a bolt of lightning.

"Could you say conclusively that the document read at the gathering was the same one you had given to Reginald three days prior?"

"Conclusively, no. Now that I think of it, I only checked that the writing and signature were as I knew them to be the earl's and that the signature on the papers had been properly witnessed by an independent individual. Which they were. So, I had no hesitation in notarizing the will." Suddenly, a look of realization spread over Kendricks's face. "Oh, dear God! Do you think Reginald changed the contents of his brother's will?"

"Yes, dear sir. I certainly do."

We sat in silence for a moment until I had an idea.

"I'm sorry to put you on the spot, old chap, but I think I should warn you that there may be a time in the very near future where either myself or Holmes might be forced to ask a great deal of you in our efforts to bring our suspect to justice. Are you in the game?"

"I've been made a fool of, Watson. As a solicitor and a notary, I take that very personally. As long as you or Mr. Holmes makes a clear request of me, I'm obligated to help. You have my word on that."

"Excellent!"

Chapter Nine:
The Pieces Fall

I arrived home at around half past two that afternoon, much to my wife's pleasure.

I had eaten a light lunch on the train so she didn't have to rush the afternoon tea for my benefit. We sat in the parlor while she finished some needlework she had been working on and though I pretended to read the afternoon newspaper, my mind kept wandering back to my conversation with Kendricks. I was uneasy and it was painfully obvious that I would not be able to think of anything else until I had related the news to Holmes.

"Dear?" I asked my wife. She looked up dutifully from her sewing and I continued. "I know it rather late in the day but do you think there is any way that I could get a telegram off to Baker Street? It's rather urgent."

"Well, if it's rather urgent, I'm sure the neighbor's boy, Conner, would be happy to run a letter over there himself," she suggested. Then added with a smile, "All you'd have to do is provide the right amount of enticement." She winked and rubbed her forefinger and thumb together in the universal symbol for monetary compensation. I gave her a knowing smile and a nod.

While I scribbled my message to Holmes, she went out the back door to call to the neighbor's wife and ask if we could borrow Conner's services for the task. I ensured to give enough details in the letter that Holmes might find it imperative to come see me that evening but not too much that the clever old boy might figure things out on his own and leave me out of the mystery solving.

I laughed as soon as I had thought it, knowing with a level of certainty that the likelihood of the latter occurring was rather high.

By the time the boy stepped into the parlor with his cap in his hand, I had the letter sealed and ready for delivery and it went into young Conner's hand accompanied by a shiny shilling.

An hour later, just as my wife was setting out the tea things, Conner returned and stood politely at the back door. She ushered him into my office where I was seated at the desk going over the Galham pathology files again and making notes on my observations.

"Did you find Mr. Holmes at the Baker Street

residence, boy?" I asked him without looking up from the papers.

"Yes, sir. I did, sir."

"Very good. Any response from him?"

"He did send a note back with me, sir," the boy replied, approaching my desk and handing me a folded piece of paper.

"Well done, young Conner. Now run along. Mrs. Watson will have a treat of some sort in the kitchen for you to have with your tea."

The boy smiled widely and made his way back to the rear of the house.

Once alone, I unfolded the paper and read its content, sighing loudly as I threw it onto the table in front of me.

"Well, that can't be good news," I heard from the doorway.

"He's figured it out."

"Just like that?"

"Indeed, my dear wife. That's our friend, Holmes. Just... like... that."

***

As my friend's note had stated, Holmes arrived at my house just in time to join me in my study for an aperitif before dinner. It had been a week since I had returned from Stratford-upon-Avon and the exact evening he had indicated I should expect his visit.

My wife had set out a small amuse-bouche of fois gras, water crackers and thinly sliced ripe figs and apricots; I poured us each a small glass of dry sherry and took a seat in my favorite armchair. Holmes sat by the open window and lit his pipe.

I had been rather concerned about his peculiar disappearance from the public house and wondered what had prompted his behavior. More importantly, having become a bit of an expert in deciphering Sherlock's strange behavior over the years, I knew his disappearance was directly linked to some clue or other he had untangled in the case. I was therefore rather curious to find out what he had discovered over the past week.

As a courtesy to my wife, Holmes and I kept our conversation for after dinner and made pleasant conversation on many other topics during the meal. Mrs. Watson was particularly occupied with the observations Sherlock made on the wide varieties of meadow plant and insect life in Stratford-upon-Avon. Having been raised in a rural county, she was completely engaged by the subject and it made me happy to watch their carefree banter at the table.

With dinner complete, we men retired to my office. I had barely shut the door before Holmes began to ramble about how he should have seen something sooner. I was secretly relieved that I wouldn't have to press him about the case; in my experience, one got a rather dull response from the detective if he felt interrogated during a conversation.

He stopped his muttering and turned to me. "It's becoming increasingly obvious that you discovered something in Stratford-upon-Avon that you're practically bursting to tell me," he said.

"Well, I wouldn't say that I'm bursting, Holmes, but I am quite sure my discovery is of significant importance to solving the case."

"Let's have it then," he snapped.

I proceeded to tell him about my suspicion that chloroform had in fact been utilized to render the Galham family unconscious prior to their murders. I explained that perhaps the clue had gone unnoticed as a result of a combination of country policing and the pathologist's inability to identify and test for the substance.

"Indeed, Watson. Tests for substances of this sort are still in its infancy, and, since a conclusion of murder and then suicide had perhaps been prematurely made by the police, the doctor would not have foreseen the need to pursue the matter."

"That was exactly my line of thinking, Holmes."

"It's a plausible one. Good job, my man." I smiled at his praise, knowing full well that there was more. "However, I think we are beyond confirming that the Galhams were victims of foul play."

I let his comment sink in, realizing he was, as usual, ahead of me in the game, before raising the subject of his hasty retreat from the town. I asked, "What happened to you in Stratford-upon-Avon? You seemed to just disappear into the night."

"It's a very strange tale, my dear Watson, but the idea came to me after you left my room. I was sitting by the window smoking my pipe and just as if a brisk wind had hit my face, the notion of what the motive behind our case might be came to me." I knew better than to interrupt him once he had started his narrative of discovery, so I took a seat by the fireplace and listened intently instead. "I wondered, could the break in at Baker Street and the subsequent theft of the manuscript have just been a smokescreen? And... if that were the case, what was its purpose? Perhaps, I thought, it was to keep us occupied with a mystery that had very little to do with the real mystery at hand. It occurred to me, Watson, that a secret as consequential as the possession of a lost masterpiece by the Great Bard himself could actually be the least of Galham House's innuendos.

"That morning, I visited the local records office and, after quite a fair bit of digging around, I found what I was looking for: the names of all the local midwives who were practicing at the time when Lady Edith, the Dowager Countess of Galham, was residing as the Countess of Galham House."

"Midwives? What in heaven's name for, Holmes?" As was to be expected, he completely ignored my question and continued his recollection.

"After sifting through that list, I found there were only three of those women still alive and living around Penstone Heath, so I visited them all in person. On my second try, I met a pleasant woman by the name of Annabel Moseley, who claimed she attended to Lady Edith on all matters of the female constitution during all the countess's years at Galham. She examined Edith regularly and had her on a very strict regimen of herbal remedies for some of the countess's health concerns. Listed prominently among them were dried berries of vitex agnus-castus, dioscorea villosa and viburnum prunifolium."

I thought about what Holmes was telling me for a moment and as I slowly began to recognize the scientific names for vitex or chaste tree berry, wild yam root and black haw, my jaw dropped almost to the floor. They were all well-known medieval herbal remedies traditionally used by midwives and herbalist to prevent miscarriage, treat a condition callously referred to as 'irritable uterus' and believed to stop uterine spasm and contractions.

"Mrs. Moseley also informed me that Lady Edith made two trips to her familial home during that time and in both instances, she returned with a newborn baby. Both hiatuses were approximately forty-two weeks long and consistent with a departure in very early pregnancy, followed by a return home shortly after giving birth. The midwife told me that aside from having her feelings a little hurt, she found nothing out of the ordinary with the practice. A lot of the older aristocratic families still follow such patterns of childbirth; in particular, leaving home.

"However, Annabel did go on to tell me one other very interesting thing. It seems that on the first of these occasions, the Countess unnecessarily delayed examinations by the midwife, even though it was customary that frequent checks on both mother and child be made to record and monitor their progress. Annabel claims that she was not able to see Mary before at least six months had passed and, by then, she claims everything was back to normal with the countess and she seemed as if she had never gone through the rigors of pregnancy and childbirth. According to the midwife, that is not uncommon with the upper-class women, though, as they are usually well fed and exercised all their lives."

"So the woman took fertility herbs and then she got pregnant. What has that got to do with anything, Sherlock?" I asked, only resorting to his first name out of complete exasperation.

"Once again, Watson, you fail in an attempt at backward reasoning. Furthermore, you haven't heard me out!"

"You mean, there's even more exciting news about the countess's childbirth habits and practices?" I asked, rolling my eyes.

"There *is* more, and the most important clue at

that. And eye rolls are not becoming of a man of your stature, Watson. Leave it for the younger generation. Now, Edith's return from the second pregnancy went a little differently. Mrs. Moseley was invited to attend the countess and her newborn child within a day of their arrival at Galham House. In her estimation, the observations she made were consistent with the normal condition of a postpartum woman and, therefore, reflective of a true and successful pregnancy and delivery."

"In other words, she has proof of Reginald's birth but not of Roger's."

"Exactly so."

"How exactly does that help our case, Holmes?" I asked, veritably begging my infuriating friend.

"Backward reasoning, Watson. The crime at the epicenter of everything is the murder of the Galhams. What was the reason for the atrocity? Reasoning backwards would go something like this: Who would stand to gain from the family's death? Was the will changed? If so, what would be the real purpose of that with the laws regarding inheritance being as defined as they are for aristocratic holdings? What content could have been in it that could change the way the pieces lay on the game board?"

"Reginald's legitimacy!" I cried.

"See? You can reason backwards."

I stood and paced. "In that case, the midwife

confirming the countess's condition wouldn't be any proof against Reginald. If anything, I'd think that question would strengthen an argument for Reginald's legitimacy."

"Not by any means, Watson! It proves Reginald is his mother's child perhaps, but Countess Edith Galham did not hold the title in her own right, her husband did. And in the case of Roger and Reginald, we have yet to confirm who their father was."

***

Before leaving my house that night, Sherlock told me another tale.

Though he had made it sound as if the question of Roger and Reginald's parentage was a question that was still up in the air, Holmes had made it his business while in Stratford-upon-Avon to find out everything that he could about the matter. As it had turned out, while I was spending the morning coming to my own conclusions in Llewelyn Kendricks's office, Holmes had been busy about town with his research. Knowing full well that his abandoning me at the inn would prompt my immediate return to London, he spent the afternoon in the village procuring an invitation for himself to an opulent garden party which Reginald Galham was to be giving that weekend.

That Saturday afternoon, he arrived impeccably

dressed at the door of Harcourt Hall and acted as escort to Lady Jessica Flora of Harcourt and Avon. Since the theft of the manuscript, Holmes had felt indebted to Lady Jessica while at the same time being convinced she might be in danger from the thief.

They went by carriage to Galham House and joined a multitude of aristocratic guests on the estate's extravagant south lawn. The last days of summer provided perfect outdoor weather for Reginald's guests and the boisterous group regaled themselves with lawn games, and excessive eating and drinking. By the time the sun had set, most of the party guests were rather intoxicated.

One by one, the visitors went upstairs and changed for dinner at the sound of the evening gong before proceeding to the drawing room for more drinks and then going in for their meal. It was a sumptuous affair but also strategically sobering as well. Afterward, the men retired to Reginald's game room and Kendricks was kind enough to remain close to Holmes so as not to isolate him from the crowd of affluent men in attendance. In my opinion, Holmes was rather capable of handling himself in any situation quite competently, but Kendricks provided him the perfect vehicle from which Holmes could conduct an in-depth observation of both his quarry and his surroundings.

It was exactly the means by which Holmes was able to make note of five matching iron trunks stacked decoratively in a corner. They were identical in every way but their size; even down to the heavy lock centered on the front. Arranged to look like a metal pyramid, the largest on the bottom to the smallest at the top, they dominated that corner of the room. A lovely Asian rug had been partially draped over them for effect.

"Rather peculiar these trunks you have over here, Lord Reginald. Rather peculiar, indeed," Holmes said loud enough for their host to hear. As he expected, Reginald immediately made his way over to Holmes and Kendricks to boast a little.

"Yes, aren't they quite," he started. "They, of course, belonged to my father. I can't recall exactly but I believe he said he brought them back with him from some war or the other. Footlockers of his command. His attendants would carry his dinnerware and other such utensils around in them. As was expected, the original contents were returned to the War Office but he was allowed to keep the boxes."

"What a remarkable story!" Kendricks proclaimed.

"If you say so," Reginald concluded with a very bored look on his face.

"Would you mind terribly if I took a closer look?" Sherlock had asked.

"Oh, not at all, but I think they're all locked and the keys have long since been misplaced. Hence, their present decorative nature."

Holmes nodded, as did Reginald before walking away to engage another man in conversation.

Holmes instinctively touched the key that resided in his jacket pocket. He stepped closer to the stack of footlockers and inspected them a little more closely and began pondering how he would manage to gain access to the strongboxes. Kendricks strolled over to the detective and offered him a glass of brandy.

"What have you come up with, Mr. Holmes?"

"A rather fascinating notion, Mr. Kendricks."

"Which is?"

Kendricks had to wait for a fairly long time before he was finally furnished with a somewhat mediocre answer. Whenever Holmes felt that the game was afoot, the old boy never gave away the players or the strategy, only instructions.

"I am going to need you to create an opportunity for me. One in which I can get to those boxes in the corner to investigate their contents. Is it possible for you to do so before, say, noon tomorrow?"

"I believe that I can come up with something."

"Perfect!" Holmes replied, smiling at the look of expectation on Kendricks's face. He touched a finger to the side of his nose and concluded, "I do not need to know how you will do it, just as you do not need to know why I need you to... for the moment at least."

Kendricks sighed, then returned the detective's knowing smile and walked out to the middle of the room.

"Ladies and gentlemen, may I have your ear, please? As you all know, next week marks the opening of the grouse season and, as is the custom in our shire, a Thanksgiving service will be held tomorrow at the village church followed by a luncheon at Harcourt Hall. The Harcourts and I insist on your presence for the festivities."

It was a checkmate move that Kendricks had made. The express invitation from a nobleman extended to a known list of guests under his peer's roof was not something to be taken lightly, especially when the heiress of said household was present and knew all those who'd been invited. It was as good as written in stone that everyone there would be engaged in the Harcourt's hospitality from ten in the morning until well after two in the afternoon. Galham House would be empty and those servants who were not off duty on Sunday would be at Harcourt Hall helping with the luncheon preparations.

Holmes had his opportunity!

***

But still the old boy kept me in suspense.

The night following dinner at my home, Holmes and I were sitting in his library at Baker

Street sipping coffee and going over the events of the case. I had been on tenterhooks the whole night and day waiting to hear about the great caper of his into Reginald's game room. Finally, it seemed he was ready and I set down the coffee cup and sat forward in my seat. He took a position by the window and lit his pipe, puffing luxuriously; no doubt to build the suspense further.

Just as he was about to tell me how he snuck into Galham House to inspect the strongboxes and reveal what he had found, there was a loud rap on the door. There was a boy at the door and we both heard the housekeeper speaking to him briefly before closing the door and making her way toward the room.

"A telegram, sir," she said, handing the folded paper to Holmes before turning to leave the room. As he read the message, my dear friend's face grew drawn and thoughtful. Suddenly he fell into a silent mood and sat gazing out the window while I could only sit and wait.

Just a few moments after Holmes had sunk into his melancholy, he just as suddenly snapped back to reality and announced loudly, "Come Watson. The game is afoot!"

Chapter Ten:
The Game is Afoot

"My dear Watson," Holmes said, "I believe we should be on our way immediately." He jumped to his feet; grabbed his coat, hat, and cane, then briskly moved out the front door to the street.

I followed as quickly as I could, being forced to make an ungraceful plunge to be able to catch the same cab as he did.

"My dear fellow," Holmes was telling the driver, "I'll double your rate if you can get me to Penstone Heath with the utmost haste and minimal delay."

"Whatever you say, sir," the driver said in a heavy Cockney accent.

The carriage leapt forward as the driver put the reins into his horses. The ringing of iron-shod hooves against the cobblestones echoed so loudly that I was barely audible over the sound.

"Holmes!" I shouted at the top of my lungs. "You'd better have a good reason for trying to get me killed tonight! My wife will *never* forgive you if you do!"

"Watson, my good man, we are going to Penstone to prevent another murder," Holmes said me.

"How in the world did you come to that conclusion? What did the telegram say?" I yelled back.

"Think, Watson!" Holmes shouted back at me. "Roger Galham's original will must have contained all the damning evidence in existence which would ruin any claim Reginald has on the family seat. Roger did this because somehow he'd managed to unravel the fact that he was the illegitimate son of the Earl Galham and Miss Harcourt's mother, the Countess Avon, and that Reginald is the son of Lady Edith, the dowager countess and the Reverend Jones! That was Roger's reasoning behind cutting Reginald out of the line of succession to the Galham title. Roger may have been a bastard as well but at least, he was his father's son; Reginald could make no such claim. That's why, considering the new light being shed on the whole affair, if the document is proven a forgery, then all of it will be going to the Harcourts because, as we already know, they are Roger's true family line by virtue of his mother. We have to get to Penstone before Reginald does something far worse than he already has."

I sat dumbfounded in my seat, across from what had to be the smartest sleuth in the Empire. The man's mind certainly worked in mysterious ways, and I could only wonder how he was able to unravel such tangled webs of deceit with what seemed to be remarkable ease.

The carriage screeched to an abrupt halt outside Harcourt Hall. The horse's hooves struck sparks as the driver sawed hard at the reins. The carriage rocked violently. Before it had time to settle, Holmes was out the door, shoving coins into the driver's hand. I jumped out of the carriage after him. I heard him shout, over his shoulder, to the driver, "Keep the change and thank you for the ride!"

***

The gate was closed for the night but after gaining access through a pedestrian entrance along the wall, Holmes and I ran straight up to the house. He stopped for a moment to look at the door, then pointed as he said to me in a soft voice, "Watson, what do you think of this?"

The door had been left slightly ajar. Very peculiar and very mysterious. "Holmes, you are ten steps ahead of me tonight. I can't even begin to fathom what you make of it, so lead the way."

"What I make of this," he continued, "is that it

would seem that there is someone in there that should not be. If that person had been invited in, they would have closed the door. So clearly, they didn't want to be heard as they entered. That means either that person is waiting for their moment, or they already took it. However, if the crime had already happened, they would have closed the door behind them as they left, to hide anything amiss. So, we're here in time," Holmes said. "Perhaps exactly on time."

"Well then Holmes, we should probably go ruin their night," I replied in a soft voice.

"Indeed. That is precisely what we shall do," Holmes said, and there was a wild sparkle in his eye.

I moved to open the door but Holmes grabbed my wrist to stop me from pushing on it. Holmes gestured to the hinges, and then examined them closely for a moment, then lightly ran his fingers over them. Rubbing his thumb and forefinger together, he seemed satisfied. He released my hand and gave me a curt nod. I pushed the door open wide enough for the two of us to pass through, and we found ourselves in the foyer. We quickly looked around but realized that there was nothing to be found on this floor. Holmes gestured to the grand stairwell.

He pulled me close and whispered in my ear, "Stay to the left edge of the stairs. These older houses have a tendency to creak. I'll stay to the right. We won't be on the runner, though, so make sure to step as lightly as you can."

I nodded my acquiescence before proceeding to the staircase. I paused and Holmes looked at me expectantly; waiting for me to take the first step. Holmes watched me and matched my step exactly. I realized he was going to step with me. That way even if we made noise, as unlikely as that was, we would only sound like one person. We took the stairs slowly and it took us almost no time at all to make our way to the top of the staircase; sometimes you have to go slow to go fast.

Holmes and I crouched, almost instinctively, for no real reason. Holmes grinned roguishly at me. We could hear voices drifting down the hall. One was deeper, and one was higher in pitch. We both came to the same conclusion, a man and a woman, before proceeding, again, in lockstep down the hall.

We got closer, and could begin to make out words; snippets of conversation. It was not a conversation that Holmes would be comfortable hearing. It was clearly a declaration of love. It made me nostalgic for my wife. It sounded very similar to the night I declared my love for her and asked for her hand in marriage. I looked over and saw the bachelor's grimace on Holmes's narrow face.

As we got closer to the room, I was suddenly forced to stop as quickly as I could. Holmes took immediate note and he stopped as well, one foot hovering inches above the ground. He looked at me inquisitively and I mimed laying down, and pointed ahead of us. Several feet ahead, against the darkened hallway, there was a human shape lying down with their arms extended out ahead of them. Based on their position, and from my time in the military, I had an instinctive notion that this someone was preparing to take a shot at the occupants of the bedroom through an opening in the cracked door.

It only took Holmes a moment to come to the same conclusion. He was in motion faster than I would have thought possible. Normally, Holmes avoids fights unless they are essential to his plan, the way sensible men avoid the plague. But in this case, neither of us had much time to lose. Stealth was no longer an option as Holmes charged toward the gunman. Hearing us, he turned and saw Holmes. In the backlighting, I could clearly see it was Reginald. The raw, unadulterated anger in his eyes told me he wasn't going down without a fight. I wanted to shout out a warning to Holmes but I didn't risk it in fear of breaking my friend's concentration.

Reginald rolled to his right to avoid the toe of Holmes's boot, and, in the process, let loose with an ear-splitting gunshot. The bullet shattered the trim right behind where Holmes had just been. Reginald, to his athletic credit, rolled straight away to his feet, only to be met by the back of Holmes's right hand. Remarkably, Reginald pivoted and struck Holmes on the side of the head with a hard elbow blow. My friend's knees buckled, giving me the clearance to lash out with my cane. I cracked it down on Reginald's arm as he leveled the gun at Holmes's chest. He cried out in unexpected pain and I swung again, this time for his knee. Reginald slipped around the cane, thus throwing me dangerously off balance. He delivered a savage kick to my previously crippled leg, and I collapsed with a grunt of real pain.

Recovering himself, Holmes delivered what should have been a crippling blow to the man's jaw. Apparently, Reginald had received training in boxing, because he turned his head and allowed Holmes's punch to merely slide across his chin. Holmes, who was no amateur himself, expected Reginald to try following up with an uppercut. He wasn't disappointed. Holmes moved his head back and caught Reginald's arm as it came up past his head. Holmes wrenched the arm around and pulled it behind Reginald's back. The man tried to pivot with Holmes but my friend's footwork was impeccable. Anticipating the move, Holmes shoved him up against the wall, pinning him there nicely.

"Watson? A hand," he said cavalierly.

"What, exactly, would you like me to do?" I asked. "You seem to have the situation quite under control."

"Your wit, as ever, Watson, is very droll. Would you be so kind as to take Reginald's other hand—" which at the time was flailing around, trying to strike Holmes "—in order to help me restrain him?"

I responded promptly, grabbing his wrist. At this point, we realized that the couple inside the room had become aware that something was amiss, ruining their moment. Forcing Reginald into the room, Holmes was able to reveal to them the cause of the fracas and what the perpetrator's intent had been for them.

"What, precisely, is going on here?" Gerald Fitzwilliam asked Reginald. The Marquis of Tach Saggart's face was flushed bright red in outrage as he waited for Reginald to explain himself.

"Ha! You should know. You of all people, you upstart bastard," Reginald spat back. Fitzwilliam grew even more red, if that was even possible.

"Don't you use that word in reference to me. Don't you dare use that type of language in front of your betters and especially in the presence of a lady! You insolent, rotten, piece of..." Fitzwilliam glanced at Lady Jessica Flora of Harcourt and Avon, and then thought better of finishing his barrage of name calling.

"Watson," said Sherlock Holmes, "perhaps we should call the constable."

"I wholeheartedly share that sentiment, old boy," said I.

Chapter Eleven:
Elementary!

When the police had finally left, Holmes and I refreshed ourselves at Lady Harcourt's request and sat by the fire in the parlor, sipping brandy while we waited for the Harcourt carriage to arrive to take us back to London.

"Holmes," I protested, "I'm still not quite sure how you figured it all out even without the crucial information I had about the murders."

"I must say that once I had managed to make a solid connection between Reginald Galham and Gerald Fitzwilliam, it was rather easy business, Watson."

"How so?" I pressed. I had to admit that the tiny piece of evidence changed nothing in my perception of the case. I was intrigued with whatever difference that information had made in Holmes's mind.

"Well, it was clear from early on that Fitzwilliam wasn't our man and Lady Harcourt would have had nothing to gain from the manuscript's disappearance unless she had intended to sell it for profit."

"Highly unlikely, considering her vast wealth and impeccable pedigree."

"Precisely!" Holmes exclaimed. He paused dramatically in front of the fire, lifted a long wispy firebrand and used it to catch a flame from the fire to light his pipe. He puffed twice and swished the stick to put out the flames, returning it neatly to its place beside the fire poker. "In the tiny web of characters that made up our mystery, there was only one left at which I could point my suspicions."

"Really, Holmes," I said, exasperated. "I do sometimes think that you make these deductions of yours up after the fact. Could the manuscript not have been stolen at random?"

"Not at all, Watson. You yourself surmised that the robbery didn't seem random and we agreed that the perpetrators must have been watching the goings on at Baker Street for quite a while to ascertain an easy access point."

"True, indeed. So how did you confirm that it was Reginald who had been behind the entire thing?"

"Well, it's as you always said, Watson. 'The proper study of mankind is man.' How many times have I heard you make this observation?" He paused again, but that was to attend to his pipe; he did not in the least way expect me to answer the question. "It was that very statement that led me into the next phase of the investigation. You see, faced with the truth about his legitimacy, Reginald was rather inclined to secure his claim to the seat of Galham. Indeed, Roger and his children were now dead, leaving him as the sole heir but if at any time the legitimacy of his claim could be challenged... then he would be stripped of title and land and perhaps even incarcerated."

"Definitely incarcerated, if it were ever determined that he'd had a hand in the murder of the entire Galham family!" I exclaimed.

"Indeed, Watson, indeed. So, Reginald had to secure his claim and he did so by getting rid of the only other two people he could think of who would be able to prove he was not the son of the old earl."

I thought about that. "His own true parents; the Dowager Countess and Reverend Jones!" I gasped. They were the only two people still alive who knew the truth and though they stood to benefit from Reginald ruling over Galham and its vast income, if put under the gun by the authorities, they would give him up as quick as a shot.

"They were murdered last night. Kendricks sent me the telegram. It was delayed on the afternoon train and was delivered after you arrived at Baker Street tonight."

"But how did you know Reginald would be

here?"

"Now that was sheer luck, my friend, but I did assume that if he'd murdered his true parents to keep his secret, the likelihood that he would be in quite a rush to execute the last move in his plan was rather elementary thinking and, as it turned out, I was right. After all, by taking out Gerald Fitzwilliam and Lady Jessica, all proof against him would have been eradicated."

"Amazing!" I proclaimed. "You truly are, but I'm sure you already know that."

"Perhaps, but there is still one small piece of the puzzle that I have yet to figure out."

"What is that, dear friend?"

"Oh, my dear Watson, it is not the question of 'what' but rather, now it is a question of 'how.'"

"Will you be able to come to a conclusion on it?"

"Considering your findings in the pathological reports of our murder victims, I am inclined to think now I will be."

Chapter Twelve:
The Truth Will Set You Free

Reginald could not believe what he had just heard.

Now, he was raging inside. He felt betrayed and lost at the thought that everything he had ever known was a lie. Upon further reflection, he realized that that was exactly what his life had been. One long string of sad lies.

"The question, 'brother,'" he said tersely, anger making his voice sound like barrels of rocks rolling down the side of a hill, "is what you're going to do about this."

"Neither of us would ever be able to hold our heads up in polite society again if any of this change gets out," Roger stated, hating that he was being faced with the types of decisions he was having to make. "It seems that the practical thing to do is to proceed as normal. No one's been hurt thus

far but, as steward of this estate, I'm sure you know that it is my moral duty to protect its longevity and to ensure that it remains in the rightful hands." Roger looked meaningfully at Reginald.

While Roger had the hot blinding anger of a Celtic warrior; Reginald had the cold, determined, calculating anger of deep winter. For him, it was a process. Steps that could be taken in order to achieve an end. Currently, all of that cold calculation was turned toward self-preservation. Reginald enjoyed a certain life, and he would be loath to give it up. The truth of their parentage would also prove to be an immovable barrier for the marriage he yearned for with Lady Harcourt.

"Roger, what the hell is that supposed to mean? You're willing to continue to support me but until when? What are my stakes in this estate now? You're no more legitimate than I am, as you well know," Reginald spluttered, his anger debilitating even his basic ability to speak.

"Brother, that's where you're wrong," Roger suddenly said forcefully. He needed Reginald to understand his position clearly and not feel any need to stir the pot further. "I can claim the paternal line of Galham, that the earl was my father. However, he was not yours."

The conversation had gone on for a while longer with each man arguing back and forth, but Roger was stalwart in his decision. The estate would continue to support Reginald in the same fashion it always had and for the rest of his life, but under no circumstances would Reginald remain in the line of succession to the title of Galham.

Going in, Roger had foreseen an argument with Reginald, but what Roger hadn't predicted was his vengeance.

***

"Listen to me, Reg," Paul said quietly, the frost in his tone managed to quench enough of the fire raging in Reginald's eyes. "We can fix this... in a way. If the will never gets changed, if the truth never gets out, then it's not really true, and we get to maintain what we have here, right?"

"I... I suppose," Reginald said. Paul Kijumbe could see that he had his work cut out for him. At the beginning, he hadn't been too sure about taking a position of valet to a second son. The prestige was certainly not comparable to that of an earl's valet. But his years in service to Lord Sutton, a merchant aristocrat, was below his station. Any member of the peerage, even a second son, was a huge leap upward in Paul's estimation and he'd taken the job. From the first day, he'd had to clean up after Reginald. Showing women out of the house through the servant's exits and even paying off a maid he'd accidentally gotten pregnant. All those things had ensured that Reginald became more and more indebted to Paul... and Paul enjoyed being in

that enviable position most of all. Even now, Reginald had come to him for a solution to the latest debacle; as it turned out, he was a servant in a house overrun by bastards.

"So, if we don't want the truth to get out, or your situation to be altered at all, all we have to do is take care of Roger, right?" Kijumbe asked.

The truth of it was no action was necessary. Roger had agreed to keep things exactly as they were; Reginald would continue to receive a salary from the estate's earnings for his lifetime, but he wouldn't inherit. That hadn't stopped Reginald's pride from being hurt, after all; the whole point was having a shot at being Earl Galham.

Reginald's being put aside by Roger was what stirred Paul into action. If Roger claimed Reginald couldn't remain in the succession to the seat of Galham, then Reginald had every right to show his brother what for.

"I... I suppose," Reginald said again. Kijumbe rubbed his face. Stirring Reginald up was clearly going to be a task. It was important that Reginald feel as strongly about the matter as Paul did if the plan was going to work.

"So how do we make them disappear, Reginald?" Kijumbe asked tersely, hoping his frustration did not show through his voice. No wonder Roger had passed Reginald over, he was such a coward!

"Well, we could..." Reginald started, but then

he paused to think a bit harder. "We could make sure they don't tell anyone else about my legitimacy," Reginald added, with a mischievous look in his eye.

"Exactly," Kijumbe said. "We make sure that he doesn't tell anyone, and we make sure that his will never gets made public. At least, not the one cutting us... I mean you, out."

"Exactly," Reginald said. "So how do we get the bugger?"

"I have a plan for that," Kijumbe said. "I'll make sure that the will never goes public. I've got a man who's aces at forging signatures. He owes me an enormous debt; he'll be able to fix up anything you need. We already know that a will has been submitted to the solicitors, but that doesn't mean it's a final one. People change their wills all the time. They have two people witness it and it's legal. When the solicitors call for the last will and testament, I'll send out the copy we have and all the signatures will pass their inspection, I promise."

"That's good. That's really good," Reginald said.

"So what will you do now?" Kijumbe asked him.

"Well... I'll take care of Roger. That'll be no problem at all," Reginald said.

"And the others too," Kijumbe responded.

"Yes. All of them."

"Good. How do you think you'll do it?"

"I can sneak in during the middle of the night and smother them in their sleep. I'll burn the damn house to the ground with them in it if I have to! That'll make it look enough like an accident," Reginald replied.

"When will you do it? We don't want to botch this at all. It will end up looking suspicious," Kijumbe said. "I can take care of the wills tomorrow. Can you have a plan ready to take care of your end in a couple of weeks?"

"Indeed, I think that will do it," Reginald replied.

***

The next day, Kijumbe walked into the Coventry Garden part of the city to find his forger, Eli Cobbs. In his days as valet to Lord Sutton, Paul had met Eli when Lord Sutton had bailed him out of a Surrey jail in exchange for Cobbs forging several Bills of Laden for him.

The man had somehow managed to get himself a position in a notary's office, most likely with the use of false references. Paul was a little intimidated by the opulent office space but, dressed in his valet's uniform and the livery of the house, he felt a little more at ease and not at all out of place. Furthermore, he was sure the man he was going to see would be able to help them with Roger's will. He walked in and greeted the receptionist.

"I'm here to see Mr. Cobbs, please."

The woman did not give Paul so much as a second look and the man was relieved for it. Shortly after she called for him, Cobbs emerged from the rear of the office.

"Cobbs! How are you mate?" he asked jovially.

"Doin' well Paul, just fine thank ye. What can I do ye for?" Cobbs replied.

"Well, hate to spoil such a lovely reunion and all, but I'm unfortunately here on some business. I was wonder'n, if ye can't come to lunch with me at the pub so we can talk?" Kijumbe replied.

"Ah... sounds serious..." Cobbs replied slowly.

"As I said, it's private and along the lines of our previous acquaintance," Kijumbe answered, keeping a smile firmly on his face.

"Wait here," Cobbs told Kijumbe, "I'll just let the clerk know I'm taking off and we can leave." When he re-emerged, Cobbs gestured to Paul to follow him. "C'mon with me this way."

They went a short distance down the road to a local place where the workers in the area often had their tea and luncheon. Paul thought it best he pay for the man's meal to ease the weight of the situation he was about to put him in. So over a hearty meal of lamb stew and brown bread, washed down with cool ale, Paul made his request to Cobbs and the forger was more than happy to oblige him. Paul handed him the original and a list of changes that he needed to be made to the document. Cobbs looked over the list carefully.

"So when can you get it done already?" Kijumbe asked Cobbs as they made their way to the exit of the pub.

"I just needed to confirm a few things," Cobbs replied happily. "But I don't think it'll be longer than a week."

"Of course, of course," Paul replied. "How about lunch again then? Next week Friday will give you a week and a half."

"Certainly we can do that. You know where to find me!" Cobbs said.

"I do. See you then."

Cobbs made to respond to the man but Kijumbe was already stepping across the street.

***

Two weeks later, Reginald was outside Galham House waiting patiently.

Finally, he heard the church bells in the distance chime midnight. He made his way silently through the groundsman's shack and out onto the lawn. There was no light for him to move by but that did not bother him, he knew the gardens well enough. As a precaution, he proceeded slowly anyway, and finally made his way to the side door of the kitchen. He opened it silently.

Once in the kitchen, managing the crowded

room proved to be a challenge... and he did not even have the pale light of the stars to guide him. He made his way slowly and carefully to the main dining room and then into the hall. As he was taking his first step toward the staircase, he transferred his weight from his left foot to his right, and felt the board groan under his weight. His heart raced and he felt the first beads of sweat form on his brow. He was no professional at this but a baser instinct took hold. He paused there, waiting for any sign of movement or alertness from the rooms above. Hearing none, he softly exhaled, not even realize he had been holding his breath.

He continued up the stairs, testing each one before sliding his foot parallel with the step to transfer his weight, thus allowing him to determine whether or not it would creak. At the top of the stairs, he crouched again in darkness, waiting to see if anyone was moving about. Once Reginald determined that he was still passing through unnoticed, he made his way to the bedroom where he knew his brother Roger and his wife Mary were sleeping.

He was rather surprised to find that the door had been left ajar but after a pause to ascertain if either Roger or Lady Mary were about the halls, he went in. He slipped in silently and ghosted his way over to the bed and swiftly administered the chloroform to Roger, but rather than waiting for it to take effect, he immediately grabbed a pillow and placed it over Roger's mouth. Roger's breathing became fitful but he did not wake up. His wife, on the other hand, became a problem as she heard her husband gasping against the pillow.

"What in the world is going on?" she asked sleepily. "Reginald? What are you doing here?"

Reginald launched himself onto the bed in an attempt to restrain his sister-in-law, but she fended him off. She struggled against him a while longer and managed to land a punch to his face. He felt something crack near his eye. She gave a muffled cry of pain. Reginald was fairly certain she had broken something in her hand from the impact.

He grabbed her wrist, forcing her hand back toward her head. She yowled and screamed against him, but he finally managed to hold the damp rag over her mouth and nose long enough for her to pass out. He backed off to a corner of the room and waited.

After he was convinced that the drug had taken effect on both his victims, Reginald approached the bed again. He reached into his pocket and withdrew the bottle of poison he had brought with him. With a dropper, he administered ten drops of nightshade orally to Lady Mary... and her body immediately began to convulse. Once he was sure that she was dead, Reginald went to the other side of the bed, threw the limp body of his brother over his shoulder and exited the room.

He left Roger by the upstairs banisters and

entered the children's nursery. Neither of the sleeping figures stood a chance of survival. Reginald's knife flicked out quickly and sliced. The boy grabbed at his throat but was unable to cry out because the knife had bitten so deep it severed his vocal cords. Reginald grabbed the younger child and made quick work of him as well. He left the children where they fell, then went back down to the groundkeeper's for a long length of rope.

For a brief moment as he walked across the lawn, Reginald wondered why he felt nothing toward sister-in-law and his nephews as he had so heartlessly taken their lives, but just as quickly, he reminded himself that his legacy was what was at stake. He wouldn't be made to pay for his mother's conniving indiscretions and lies; it wasn't his fault he wasn't Earl Galham's son. He would end Roger's craven vendetta against him for good and then there would be no one left to treat him like a useless hanger-on.

Back upstairs, he made his way to Roger's still body, put the noose around his neck and tightened it as far as it would go. He tied off the remainder of the rope to the balcony railing, then in one steady motion, he lifted and heaved Roger's body over the edge. The rope snapped tight and swayed sickeningly in Reginald's night vision. If Roger was not dead before, and Reginald was pretty sure he was, then he certainly was now.

Chapter Thirteen:
The Conclusion

"Life is infinitely stranger than anything which the mind of man can invent." —Sherlock Holmes

The next morning, we had all gathered in Kendricks's office at Holmes's request.

He had invited the two arresting constables from the night before so that they could take a proper statement. In reality, Holmes was finally ready to deliver his version of what he thought might be the best explanation for the series of events our latest case had put us through.

Lady Jessica of Harcourt and Avon was there; understandably, however, her parents were absent. They were now the inheritors of the Galham Estate and all its holdings and the legalities were overwhelming for them. She sat demurely beside her new fiancé, Gerald Fitzwilliam, who I was pleased to see was as doting as he was expected to be. I felt sorry for them that their monumental engagement should have to start like this, especially after having admired each other in secret for so many years.

Llewelyn Kendricks was, as always, the ever-gracious host. He'd seen to ensuring there were comfortable seats provided for everyone and refreshments in abundance, though I did not think any of us were in a mood for it.

As soon as we had all arrived, we took our seats and Holmes stepped out in front of us. His pipe was firmly held between his lips but out of courtesy to the police and Lady Harcourt, he had not lit it. As we sat in anticipation, the detective took a few moments to slowly pace back and forth before us. I knew he was doing his best to sort out the series of events in his mind and formulate a plan for how he would deliver his narrative. Soon, he began to address us all.

"Welcome, everyone. I am particularly relieved to announce that we have come to the conclusion of our game and now it is only right that I lay the facts out before you as Watson and I have deduced them, for you have all indeed been players in the game.

"However, as I had discussed last night with my dear friend, Dr. Watson, this caper has mostly been about the 'hows' of the case rather than the 'whys.' The reasons were basal, instinctual, driven by pure self-preservation on Reginald's part and these are emotions we all too clearly understand as human beings. As members of civilized society, we keep them at bay, at an arm's length, but for some, they remain within easy reach still.

"How Reginald started this whole palaver was with the murder of his brother, Roger Galham, and his family. When Reginald had learned from Roger during a family squabble over his ridiculous spending habits that he was the bastard son of the reverend and not the Earl of Galham's son at all, he lost his mind in a fit of rage."

The account of how Roger and his family were murdered were gruesome enough for Miss Harcourt to succumb to her feminine sensitivities, but, for one reason or another, Holmes felt it important, especially for the constables present, for us all to understand the ruthlessness that had been employed in the act. Holmes held nothing back.

Holmes was silent after his retelling and stood before us, slowly shaking his head. He walked over to a table that was covered with a white sheet in the corner of the room and pulled the sheet off throwing it to the ground. There were three metal boxes with matching locks laid out side by side on the table. The smallest one first, the largest one last. Iron keys lay in front of the first and second but the third had none.

Holmes lifted the first key and turned it in the lock. The lid of the box rose easily and Holmes withdrew from it the altered last will and testament of Roger Galham. He threw it down on the table, disgusted, and stepped away, pacing in front of us again.

"Once the family had been murdered, and the false will was read and accepted, the pathology and police investigations closed, and the funerals conducted, Reginald was free and clear to assume his new position. There weren't a great many more obstacles set in his way. What he foolishly hadn't accounted for was Paul Kijumbe's treachery.

"As soon as Reginald discovered that Miss Harcourt had found the manuscript and removed it from the Galham House library, he sent Kijumbe to steal the document from my Baker Street apartments. To ensure the secret of Reginald's heritage remained safe, it was imperative that the William Shakespeare play never be properly authenticated. If it were ever found to be real, then the rumors of an indiscreet affair between Lady Anne Galham and the Great Bard could possibly be confirmed, and, if that were the case, then the question would be: Why would such a precious belonging of the Avon's turn up in the Galham Library? It would have been there because Countess Avon, Roger's mother, gifted it to Edith Galham for graciously accepting Roger into her home and allowing him the protection of his real father, the Earl of Galham."

At that point, the detective moved toward the table again. He picked up the second key and placed it into the lock on the second box. Again the lock sprang open easily and the lid of the box rose. Sherlock reached into the box and when his hand emerged, he held in it the stolen manuscript of the missing Shakespeare play.

"Earlier today, I asked several document and Shakespeare experts from all over the city to come here to Mr. Kendricks's office to take a look at this manuscript. There were eight experts, to be exact. Among them was Alexander Richardson the Third of Sotheby's auction house, a rather renowned authority on Renaissance books and literature. According to Mr. Richardson, the document is as authentic as any other Shakespeare manuscript he had had the honor to appraise or auction. He further commented that it could perhaps be the most valuable he has seen to date due to its pristine condition and the fact that it is proof of something scholars have known for years but have been unable to prove. You see, every famous artist was once a beginner, an apprentice, a novice before they were ever a professional. Therefore, it stands to reason that their more crude or unfinished attempts at their craft and their earliest completed works are out there in the world for us to discover. This is just one of such."

In conclusion, Holmes mercilessly dropped the priceless manuscript on the table in front of its box and moved on.

"Paul Kijumbe, the valet, as it turned out, was incapable of keeping his mouth shut and had been known for slandering his previous employers in the pubs of south London for years. I had a notion that the habit would not have been lost, considering Reginald should have supplied more than enough material to gossip about. It wasn't hard to find him and it didn't take long before the story of the key came out one night at the bar. You see, Paul, the instigator, had made sure that Reginald would never betray his role in the plot by stealing the key to one of the strongboxes. A box that even Reginald himself was unaware was occupied, a box that held the clue to his absolute destruction. Because unbeknownst to Reginald, the new Earl of Galham, his accomplice had not destroyed Roger's original will.

"The key for that box was kept so closely on Kijumbe's body that Dr. Watson and I had to relieve the man of his shirt to find it. But find it, and retrieve it, we did. After he woke up on the streets and realized the key was gone, Paul Kijumbe was inclined to make a hasty retreat from both the capital city and Warwickshire county, but I took it upon myself to have him detained at Scotland Yard for possible involvement in the murder of a peer of the realm. And that, dear friends, brings us to the last of our three strongboxes."

Sherlock made his way across the room again and stood before the table. He reached inside his sport jacket and from the inside left breast pocket, he retrieved a key that was identical to the two he had previously used to open the other boxes on the table. He held it up for all of us to see before slipping it into the lock and turning it. Again, the lock sprang open without hesitation and he reached inside.

The document that Holmes produced from the box was not easily recognizable. No one present in the room had ever laid eyes on it before. Holmes realized quickly that the suspense was being ruined by the fact that we had no realization of what he was holding up.

"Come on now, friends. You are all supposedly intelligent people here. There was one more item of interest that remained missing from the equation."

After a brief pause, it was Kendricks who offered a response; and it was the correct response to Holmes's challenge.

"The original, unaltered copy of Lord Roger's last will and testament," he announced.

"You've got it!" Holmes announced, throwing the pages down on the table. He picked up the last iron key and raised it up high for all to see.

"On the day that Watson and I had relieved Mr. Kijumbe of the possession of this key, I had not one clue as to where it fit into the whole mystery but I knew it was very important. Why else would the rogue carry it so closely on his person?"

I cringed, remembering again where we had located it on Kijumbe's body.

"It wasn't until the night at Galham House

when Reginald told me they were old army footlockers that belonged to his father, the previous Earl Galham, that it fell into place. The boxes, as you can see, are untarnished; not a nick or much of a scratch on them. The locks sprang free as smoothly as if they were made quite recently and so too was true of their hinges. That is only because they were only made weeks ago by the blacksmith, Mr. Tyler, who resides in Penstone Heath. Mr. Tyler was kind enough to evaluate the boxes for me, after I had removed them from Lord Reginald's possession, and gave me full confirmation that they were indeed his work. To prove his statement, he fashioned copies of the keys for box numbers one and two for me that very day. As you can all see, the keys worked perfectly.

"It was at that point that I became undoubtedly sure that not only had Reginald altered and forged his brother's will, he had also planned and executed the murder of the Galhams and unrightfully acquired the seat and property of the earldom under false pretenses. In addition to those crimes, he also had Kijumbe murder the Dowager Countess and Reverend Jones, his own mother and father. In doing so, he ensured that the valet's hands were just as dirty as his own and he also eradicated any further possibility that his claim on Galham could be disproved; all this, in one fell swoop.

"The news of the murders led Watson and myself to Harcourt Hall the very next night and, just as I had suspected, Reginald was there ready and waiting to eliminate the last threat, Miss Jessica Harcourt. Fitzwilliam falling victim to the lead in his gun would only have been a bonus, because of how much Reginald hated the man. After all, Fitzwilliam, though a man with land and a title, was from a family that made their money from their holdings in America. Reginald considered Marquis Fitzgerald to be an upstart and a nouveau riche. Also, with Lady Jessica gone, there would be not one single person alive in Penstone Heath who could lay a stronger claim to the Earldom of Galham than himself; the illegitimate son of a county parson."

***

With the case concluded, Holmes saw no need for us to linger in Stratford-upon-Avon.

I assumed he had grown quite bored of the place and I knew for a fact that country living had never appealed to him at all. As we sat in our compartment on the train back to London, he spread out a considerable collection of weeds, flowers and leaves which he had gathered in the meadows across Warwickshire and pressed carefully in a book he carried.

"What's that then?" I asked curiously.

"As it turns out, Watson, I think I may have picked up an appetite for botany. It is remarkable the things that plants are capable of, the effects they can have on the human body. I may have cost myself and my experiments dearly by overlooking their properties and so, I think I shall take up a study of it."

"Very relaxing work, botany," I replied. "Even as a doctor, I can say it is much like the study of man; appearances are almost always deceiving and the truth one finds as a result of the study is always much more strange than anything you could possibly have made up."

Holmes laughed and returned his specimens to the safety of the pressing pages.

"It's as you've always said, my dear Watson..."

"What have I always said, Holmes?"

"The proper study of mankind is man."

"Indeed, Holmes. Indeed."

The End

About the Authors:

J.R. Rain is an ex-private investigator who now writes full-time. He lives in a small house on a small island with his small dog, Sadie. Please visit him at www.jrrain.com.

Chanel Smith was born and raised in Los Angeles, California. She has since moved to Portland, Oregon, where she lives with her husband and two dogs. When not writing, she spends her time training dogs, hiking, biking and anything else that will get her outside in nature. Please visit her at: www.chanelsmithbooks.com.

Made in the USA
San Bernardino, CA
10 December 2017